Anonymous

Vicissitudes of a Gentlewoman

Vol. III

SALZWASSER
VERLAG

Anonymous

Vicissitudes of a Gentlewoman

Vol. III

Reprint of the original, first published in 1863.

1st Edition 2022 | ISBN: 978-3-37500-339-5

Verlag (Publisher): Salzwasser Verlag GmbH, Zeilweg 44, 60439 Frankfurt, Deutschland
Vertretungsberechtigt (Authorized to represent): E. Roepke, Zeilweg 44, 60439 Frankfurt, Deutschland
Druck (Print): Books on Demand GmbH, In de Tarpen 42, 22848 Norderstedt, Deutschland

VICISSITUDES

OF

A GENTLEWOMAN.

IN THREE VOLUMES.

VOL. III.

LONDON

1863.

VICISSITUDES

OF

A GENTLEWOMAN.

CHAPTER I.

SNOW had fallen deeply one night shortly after Christmas. Janet stood looking out of the window after breakfast. The white covering hung over every object.

"How purely white everything looks," said Janet. "When I was a child I used to think that the snow was like the icing on the top of a wedding-cake."

"What an extremely unpoetical idea! I thought your childish imaginings were much more sublime than about something to eat."

"They were sometimes extremely visionary—I don't think they were sublime; and don't you know that there is but a pest between the sublime and the ridiculous?"

"It's bitterly cold." Mrs Darrel drew near the fire, and put on more wood.

"The dog does not seem to find it cold; he has just rolled in the snow, and is shaking himself; he looks like a bear," said Janet.

"Which dog? Faust?"

"Yes."

"Poor old fellow, he likes the cold. We'll take him out presently."

"Edward, are you going out to-day?" asked Mrs Darrel.

"Yes, mother. Are not you? It is cold, but the air is very still."

"I shall be engaged this morning with one or two people who want to see me; then I want to see those new people who have come into the cottage in the lane; I hear they are badly off. You had better go out while the sun shines; Stephen can drive you."

"Why should not Janet drive me in the little pony-carriage? Can you drive, Janet?"

"I don't know. I have never tried since I was very little."

"I'm sure you can; and the pony is very quiet. We'll order it to be ready in half an hour."

"Oh! Mr Darrel; but suppose I should upset you!"

"I don't think you *can* upset the little pony-carriage; and as to the pony, he has never been known to run away, he is of a meditative turn of mind, and very much prefers standing still."

Mrs Darrel looked up. She could see as far ahead as most people; but where her son was concerned she could not bear to say nay to any arrangement which afforded him even a temporary pleasure. She liked Janet, and understood the young girl's character tolerably well. She was perfectly certain that Janet would not manœuvre to become Mrs Darrel. She felt pretty sure also that there was little danger of Janet's becoming involved in an attachment, which Mrs Darrel herself would be the first to check. To do Mrs Darrel justice, however much she might idolize her son, she would not on his account have risked Janet's peace of mind. Some people called her a proud, stern woman; towards some she had a haughty manner, but she had a kind, generous heart. Strange that the thought never occurred to her that her son's happiness might be endangered.

Janet came into the room with her bonnet on.

"My dear, are you wrapped up warmly? You will find driving colder than walking. Those gloves are not nearly warm enough."

"They are woollen and thick, Mrs Darrel."

"Not nearly warm enough for driving in on such a day as this; there has been an intense frost during the night. Ring the bell. You shall have a pair of mine."

The servant came.

"Tell Harris to bring a pair of my driving-gloves, warm ones."

Harris came with a pair of leather gloves with fur on the backs.

"There, Janet! now I think you may venture; but tuck your veil inside your bonnet-strings, and keep it down tight."

Stephen put his master into the

little carriage, and gave Janet the reins and whip.

“Give the pony his head, Miss, don’t hold him up so tight.”

“Which way shall we go?” said Janet.

“Through the lanes and across the common,” said Mr Darrel.

The pony trotted on briskly, and Faust ran by the side.

“Should we have time to go as far as Derwent, and get those books that Mrs Darrel wanted, before it gets very cold?” asked Janet.

“What time is it now?”

“Twelve. I think the church clock struck a few minutes ago.”

“It is seven miles to Derwent, and the pony will be more than an hour going. Yes, we shall have plenty of time. Make him go on faster.”

Janet touched him with the whip.

“Now tell me what you see,” said Mr Darrel.

“We’re passing a cottage; your nurse’s cottage I think it is; there are some most wonderful icicles hanging from the eaves, they must be more than a foot long, and they look like daggers of crystal, and are showing all the prismatic colours in the sun-light."

"Well?"

"Well, coming down the hill there is a woman in a red shawl or cloak, and a donkey with panniers. Faust is going up to the donkey; from the way he is sniffing about there must be something to eat in the panniers. The woman is frightened. Call Faust away, Mr Darrel."

Mr Darrel whistled to the dog, who returned to his master, and the woman stood curtseying, and saying that "She were always terrible afeard of dogs."

"We must be near the gate just before we come to the common."

"We are, and some children are running to open it."

"How many?"

"Three."

The gate was opened, and Mr Darrel threw out some half-pence.

"What children are they?"

"A little rosy boy and girl, and a tiny child with them."

Mr Darrel was silent for a little time then he said,—

"Janet, I wonder whether I have any real idea of what colour is? I only compare it to sound. Do you, who can see, ever find any affinity between colour and sound?"

"I dare say every one has certain associations with certain colours, I don't know that it amounts to thinking of an affinity; but that may be in my case because I have not thought much about it."

"Now I will tell you some of my fancyings; tell me whether you think they have conveyed any notion of colour. Red, for instance; I fancy it must be something very intense and powerful, and positive, like the sound of a trumpet. I always connect red with the sound of a trumpet, and with no other instrument. I have another likeness for it, a perfect fifth. *Now*, Janet?"

"Red *is* like the sound of a trumpet, but I had never thought of it before."

"It must be a glorious colour."

"It *is* a glorious colour. But you can't use much of it."

"Why not?"

"Would you like a concert of nothing but trumpets?"

"Then there is pink, and cherry-colour, and crimson, and scarlet, and maroon, what are they? The diminuendo and crescendo of red? They are not distinct colours, are they?"

"No, not different colours; pink, cherry-colour, crimson, and maroon are the diminuendo and crescendo of each other; I don't think scarlet is, it seems to me different."

"How? Which is the sound of the trumpet?"

"Scarlet."

"And crimson?"

"Not so grand as scarlet; perhaps more like the sound of a bugle."

"Janet, you are understanding me, and are making me understand what I wish."

"Blue,—what do you fancy blue is like?"

"A minor third, or the sound of a flute."

Janet remained silent.

"Why don't you speak? Isn't that at all like blue?"

"I was thinking, you know, that all these likenesses are new to me."

"I always associate blue with something sweet, touching, perhaps, but weak."

"Certainly a flute may be that. I don't like people who play the flute."

"Why?"

"I always think of mild young men petted by mammas and maiden aunts, and beguiling the time in long evenings with little doleful airs on a flute."

"That's the self-same idea, weakness."

"Then your other simile, the minor third."

"Rather sad—"

"Wrong, wrong, blue is the loveliest, brightest, most ethereal, most heavenly colour."

"We don't understand each other about blue as well as we did about red, do we?"

"Not quite; I see the analogy to the flute, but not to the minor third."

"We'll talk it over again some day."

"Then there's yellow—what is yellow like?"

"Oh! I can almost feel yellow. It is

sunshine and warmth, and light and heat; I don't think I know any musical instrument to which I can liken it. It feels to me more like a quality of tone than anything else, except that I always connect it with a major third."

"It's all right about light, and heat, and sunshine; but I don't see why you should think of a major third."

"Perhaps I can't explain intelligibly, never having seen it; but I fancy it must be a very important colour, but not so grand or powerful as red; is that right?"

"Yes, I think it is."

"Well, then, I fancy it must hold much the same position as a major third does in harmony?"

"What do you think white is like?"

"White and black are not colours, are they?"

"No, I suppose not, but we need not be so *very* correct; it is quite as likely that you should have some idea of your own about white and black as about real colours; they *are* colours to you."

"White is like unisons on the key-note."

"Yes,—now black?"

He was silent a moment.

"If I had ever seen, I should say black must be like blindness, nothing discernible but by sound or touch."

"Oh! Mr Darrel, forgive me."

"Forgive you, Janet; what for? I began the conversation; you could not foresee whither it would lead. But I was thinking how terrible blindness must be to those who have ever seen!"

Janet remained silent.

"To me it is merely that I am conscious that others possess a sense which I have not. Did you ever try to conceive another sense, what it might be like, Janet?"

"Yes, but I never could."

"Now you may pity your blind friend less."

* * * * * * * *

"That must be Derwent," said Janet. "How quickly we must have come!"

"Do you often go to Derwent?"

"No, I was never there but when I went to the concert with Mrs Platt and met you and Mrs Darrel."

They got the books for Mrs Darrel,

and turned homewards; the winter's sun was getting low as they approached Eckington.

"Don't you smell wood smoke? The women are making up their fires to get their husbands' suppers."

"I like it; there it is, curling up above those dark firs."

They drove on a little farther. There was the sound of children's voices.

"Now tell me what you see."

"There is a thatched cottage, the door is open, and I can see in; there is a fire blazing on the hearth, gleaming out through windows and door, and lighting up the inside of the room. There is a great kettle hanging over the fire, and the children are sitting round. There! the mother has come; now she is looking into the kettle. What a powerful picture it would make; the dimness outside, the glowing light in the room, the little dusky figures against the fire-light, and the light thrown, as it is, on the little girl with the baby on her lap, sitting in the chimney-corner! It looks so comfortable; one's beau-ideal of an English cottage home."

"I have no doubt but that it does; the half-light must favour the illusion; it resembles the 'good old times' we were talking of the other day with Mr Selwyn."

They drove on without speaking for some time.

"Do you remember the day we first met in Eckington church?"

"Yes, I was just thinking of it. I was waiting for Tom, and I wandered on by myself, and found the door of the church open, and I stood looking and wondering at the colours thrown by the sun on the pavement from the east window. I don't think that I ever saw anything so beautiful."

"Because you were a child."

"And I don't think that I ever enjoyed any music so much."

"A proof that what I said was true. I myself have improved since then, and you have heard music better than mine. But you were a child, and had heard none before. It is the first sip of the cup of pleasure which is the sweetest; perhaps the first sorrow which is the most bitter. Is it not so, Janet?,"

But Janet did not answer. They were near home, and the rest of the way they drove on in silence.

CHAPTER II.

A LETTER for Janet from Mr Platt; it came the morning after her drive to Derwent with Mr Darrel.

"Mr Platt thinks that I shall forget that my holiday is drawing to a close," said Janet. "He reminds me that his school opens on Monday."

"Don't you think he would give you a few days longer? I'll write and ask him," said Mrs Darrel.

"No, Mrs Darrel, thank you, I should not like to ask it."

"Why not? The rest will do you good. It won't put Mr Platt to any inconvenience. Let him give the children an extra week's holiday."

"No, thank you; I'm very much obliged to you for wishing me to stay, and for having invited me at all. I've enjoyed being here very much; but I *must* go on Monday."

It was such a bright, honest face which looked up at Mrs Darrel; she could not bear to think of her returning to her life of toil.

"Janet, I *shall* write to Mr Platt; there is no reason why you should not stay another week; a month is not too long a holiday to give you. Mr Platt may think himself fortunate to get such a governess."

"No, Mrs Darrel, please don't write to him."

"Why not? You must give me some valid reason why I should not."

Janet hesitated a moment.

"I don't know whether you'll understand me, because you have never been so circumstanced. When I asked Mr Platt to let me be his school-mistress he said that it was not a situation for a lady, and that I should soon tire of it; but I was very glad to take it; I was not sufficiently educated to take a good situation then, though I hope I shall be some day. If you were to write, I know that Mr Platt would not refuse to grant me the extra holiday; but I would rather not ask it. As long as I am the mistress of his school I wish to abide by the usual regulations, and not to seek favours because I happen to have been born to a different position. That would not be fair. I take Mr Platt's situation for my own convenience; my antecedents are nothing to him. As long as I take his salary I am his school-mistress, nothing more; I don't want to trade on my antecedents."

There was some justice, and an immense deal of pride, in what Janet said. It was so precisely what Mrs Darrel would herself have felt and done under the circumstances, that she became increasingly interested in the young girl.

"I dare say it is very incomprehensible to you, Mrs Darrel, and you may think me very foolish; perhaps, too, you think that I am making a small matter of ridiculous importance, and that it cannot be of much consequence whether I go on Monday or stay a week longer."

Mrs Darrel was resolved to make another attempt to keep Janet; she was so much improved, and the weary, harassed look had left her face; a little longer rest would be good for her.

"I quite understand you, Janet, perhaps I should do the same myself. You and I have many feelings in common."

Janet looked pleased.

"But, Janet, you are worth more to Mr Platt than a common school-mistress; therefore, it is no favour if he grants you a little longer holiday; it is only the just pay due to your services."

"But, Mrs Darrel, a common school-mistress is all that he requires; it is all that is necessary for the Stoke children. If I am something different, yet choose to take the situation which he has to offer, that is my look to; I must not expect him to pay for that which he does not want. That's what makes people afraid to employ poor ladies; people think that they shall be expected to let them off something, and to grant all manner of favours, which are very inconvenient, in consideration of 'has beens.'"

All this time Mr Darrel had been silently going on with his breakfast. He had turned from his mother to Janet, and from Janet to his mother, as each spoke, following their voices; but he had said nothing. There was a shadow on his face; he was generally cheerful, but the bright look was quite gone.

"Edward, have *you* nothing to say?" asked Mrs Darrel.

"About what?"

"About Janet's going."

"She has decided for herself."

He rose, felt his way to the fire, and sat down, leaning his head against the chimney-piece.

Mrs Darrel looked inquiringly at her son. A servant came in to say that one of the people whom she had appointed to see had come. Mrs Darrel looked at her watch; it was ten o'clock; she never kept any one waiting a minute after the appointed time; so she left the room.

Mr Darrel remained seated by the fire, with his head resting against the chimney-piece. Janet wanted to ask him about some music, but she felt that she could not, though she did not know why. He did not speak to her, and something prevented her speaking to him. She remained for a few minutes, watching the man clearing the snow from the path, then she went to her own room and wrote a note to Mr Platt, telling him that she would return on Monday. She put on her bonnet; she would post the letter herself, and have a walk that bright morning. Then she recollected that Mrs Darrel had spoken of being engaged all the morning; she thought that perhaps she ought not to have gone out alone; Mr Darrel might like a companion in his drive. She went to the post-office, and then turned back instead of walking further.

When Mrs Darrel returned to the breakfast-room some two hours after she had left it, she found her son still sitting by the fire as before.

"Edward!"

He did not answer.

"Are you not going out?"

"I don't know."

"Where is Janet?"

"Gone out."

"Why did not you go for a drive, and take her?"

"Why not? I scarcely know myself."

"I don't think she *can* be gone out."

"I heard her go to her own room; she has been writing to Mr Platt, I know; then I heard her cross the hall and go out. Don't you think I know her step? There she is."

There were footsteps in the hall; in a moment Janet appeared, fresh and glowing from her walk.

"Where have you been?" asked Mrs Darrel.

"To the post-office."

"You need not have gone yourself; we have always letters to send."

"I was intending to have a walk, and then I thought—" and Janet stopped short in the middle of her sentence.

Mr Darrel finished it for her. "You thought that I should want a drive, and remembered that my mother spoke of having some engagements this morning, and so you came back to see whether you could not use your eyes to amuse the blind man."

"I *did* come to see whether you wanted to go for a drive; but there will be scarcely time before luncheon; I did not think it had been so late."

Janet left the room to take off her bonnet.

Mr Darrel threw himself back in his chair; his hand grasped the arm. Some passion was struggling for the mastery, and an indomitable will said that it should be crushed.

"Edward!"

"Mother."

For one moment she *would* not believe; then she understood all. Poor mother! hitherto, whatever had been the trouble, she had been able to comfort him; even in the great affliction of his blindness she had been his solace, now she was powerless.

They both remained silent. There was a conflict going on in the mother's mind; and then she bent forward and kissed his forehead.

"Ask her, Edward. You shall have my blessing."

"No, mother; she does not love me. I'll go out for a drive with Stephen."

Mr Darrel went with Stephen.

His mother went to her room, and walked up and down, up and down, and stopped now and then to look at the picture over the fireplace. Why had she not foreseen this in time? Why had she invited Janet? Would that have prevented it? Then she went back in memory years, years, to the day when Janet had first come to her house, a little girl, leading her blind son. Then there was Janet's visit to Dr Thorpe, and then — then — Edward had loved Janet long; perhaps he had only now become aware of his feelings; she saw it all now. Well! she loved Janet herself. The obstacle her son placed between himself and Janet was not his blindness, but—that she did not love him. How could he know that if he had not asked her? Janet was not the kind of girl to betray her feelings; she was very honourable also; perhaps this was an additional reason why she had been so determined to go on Monday. Then the Higgins family rose up before Mrs Darrel's mental eye; not very pleasant people to be connected with! Then as a contrast to the unpleasant relations rose the vision of Janet herself, as she had come in bright and fresh from her walk an hour before, and—and—of her son's happiness. Edward had said, "No, mother, she does not love me." It was not like a Darrel to venture nothing. Then came the picture of him, as he looked when she had returned to the breakfast-room. A thrill of pain went through the mother's heart; at that moment perhaps it did not proceed entirely from feeling for her son; there might be a little sorrow for herself, a sigh for a past state of things which would never return. Those two had stood alone in the world; they had been all in all to each other. Day by day, as she planned and acted, her son's happiness was constantly kept in view. His blindness increased her love, and she watched him and ministered to him with the redoubled gentleness and thoughtfulness which finds its place in a woman's heart when her idol needs it from misfortune or infirmity. Mrs Darrel *was* an idolater, and her idol was her son. She would have been his slave, gladly, happily, so that she might be *the* one to whom he looked for happiness, so that she might reign supreme. For the future she would be only second—not second in the eyes of the world, for which, by the by, she cared but little; Eckington Manor was her own, there she would always reign supreme, and Janet was not the woman to try to depose her—but she would be second in his heart; in that son's heart whom she had watched over, and loved, and cherished for years, years, ever since she had been left alone a young widow, in that old house, and the tiny baby in her arms was what made her care to live. She stopped from walking up and down the room, and sat down by the fire with her hands in her lap. It hardly looked like Mrs Darrel sitting there; the attitude suggested irresolution. So she remained for some time. The fire burnt low; mechanically she bent forward, and put on some wood from the basket by her side; it blazed brightly, and the flame threw a glow on the picture over the fireplace; it made Mrs Darrel look up. Then she resumed her walk, up and down the room, glancing now and then at the picture. *He* had been an only son. Had his mother felt as she was feeling? But *he* was not blind; *he* had never required the watchful care which she had bestowed on *her* son, and *his* mother, the mother of the picture's original, had had a husband's heart to cling to. Up and down, up and down that room she walked, stopping every now and then as though movement checked her thoughts, and then on again as though she would gladly escape thought. Then came the remembrance of her son and Janet, as they returned from their drive to Derwent; she had rarely seen his face so lit up with happiness. Why, after all that she had done for him, in the face of all that she would sacrifice for him, should she shrink from this? But this was the greatest of all. It might be. Was not the happiness it offered him greater? The sacrifice was proportioned to the happiness. She had said, "Ask her, you shall have my blessing." The die was cast. But he had said, "No, she does not love me," and so he would be silent; she knew that he would. How could he know that Janet did not love him? He could not, he did not. Faint heart—faint heart! Not like a Darrel! Now Mrs Darrel quickened her step, and her lip was compressed; it was at the bare idea of her son's love being rejected; and she laughed a short, scornful laugh. Janet *did* love him; that was the reason of her choosing to leave on Monday; quite right, she liked the girl. Now what was to be done? Edward would not speak. She would. She walked up and down a little longer. The conflict was over now. Most women's minds are flexible. Mrs Darrel turned to the new aspect of things; she had been startled, she had never dreamed of her blind son loving any one but herself. Need she regret it? Would he not want some one to love—some one to love him, to care for him, when she was gone? There was a knock at the door. Luncheon was ready. Mrs Darrel went to the glass and re-arranged her cap and collar; she never liked to appear before her household with the slightest derangement of toilette manifest. Then she went down-stairs.

Janet was sitting by the fire, reading.

"I'm sorry you've spent a solitary

morning, Janet, but it could not be avoided. Now come and have some lunch." Mrs Darrel put some cold fowl on a plate for her.

Janet came to the table; she looked towards Mr Darrel's place as though she was surprised at his not being there.

"Edward has gone out with Stephen; I don't think he will return just yet, so we had better not wait for him."

She had never before spoken of him as Edward to Janet, but always as Mr Darrel.

"What have you been doing? Have you been very lonely?"

"Lonely! no, not at all. I had a letter to write after breakfast, then I went to the post-office," and here Janet hesitated, and her colour rose; she had returned thinking that Mr Darrel would want his drive; she knew that he liked some other companion than Stephen; after all, he had gone out without her; he did not want her; she felt as if she had done something improper, something bold, something which she ought not to have done. Her motive had been pure and kind. Her embarrassment passed in a minute, and then she said, "I looked over some music which Mr Darrel was speaking of last night, and I tried some of it; and then I took a book and read by the fire, and that is the history of my morning."

"And so you think you *must* go on Monday."

"Yes, my letter was to Mr Platt to tell him that I would return."

"You and I have never had a walk together, Janet; if you'll bear with an old woman as a companion, we'll have a walk after luncheon. There will be plenty of time before it becomes very cold."

Janet looked pleased, and said that she should like it.

"If you won't take any more, we'll put on our bonnets at once; we shall have the longer walk before the sun sets."

Janet ran up-stairs. Mrs Darrel could hear her singing to herself, through the passages, and in her room, a fragment of an air which her son had been teaching her.

They were soon equipped. They went through the shrubbery; the ground was hard and crisp.

"I have never been here since the day I first saw you," said Janet.

"When you were a little girl, and were Edward's guide, when Stephen had forgotten the hour. I remember it; but we are not going through that little gate."

They turned down another path, and passed through a gate, then through a plantation of larches, and then out on to the common. They walked on for some time without speaking. In the hedge which bounded the plantation, growing on some old wood, Janet spied some scarlet lichens; she stopped to gather them. Mrs Darrel had walked on. Janet ran after her.

"Look! are they not beautiful?" She held up the tiny cups.

Mrs Darrel said "Yes," mechanically. Generally she would have admired them as much as Janet did; now her mind was preoccupied. She was not the woman to shrink from difficulties; but now she walked on, and knew not how to begin; yet she had made up her mind to speak to Janet, and had taken her that walk with the intention of doing so before they returned.

"Do you like Stoke?" The question was asked abruptly, after a long silence.

"The place or the people, do you mean? It is a pretty little village, no one *could* dislike it; as to the people, there are none whom *you* would consider visitable but the Platts; *I* know every one, of course. They all behave very well to me, and Grace makes me very comfortable."

"You have not said whether you like it."

"Have I not? Yes, I like it as well, I suppose, as I should like most places." There was a little sigh; it said, "I can't be with those I love best; therefore all places are alike to me; or if not quite alike, yet I care less about external surroundings than I should do under other circumstances."

The sigh did not escape Mrs Darrel.

"How long shall you remain in Mr Platt's situation?"

"I hardly know."

"Have you no plans for the future?"

"Wishes many—plans I can hardly call them. For the present it seems that I must plod; and why not? I have been fairly successful." Janet spoke cheerfully; she generally put things in the pleasantest way. "After all," she continued, "it is impossible to plan much, at least *I* find it so; something always happens to set one's plans aside."

It was of no use beating about the bush. Mrs Darrel must speak plainly, or her morning's walk would be useless.

They walked on in silence a little further.

"Janet," said Mrs Darrel, "you are a good girl; you were right in wishing to go back on Monday; I understand it all now, but you need not go back. Janet—my son loves you—I only knew it this morning. He should have been here instead of me—but—it may be—it *must* be his blindness which makes him shrink back, which makes him think his love not worth a woman's acceptance; but he would make any woman happy, Janet; for he has made his mother happy."

Mrs Darrel had made a great effort to speak, she was agitated, and with the last words her voice faltered. She believed that she was bringing happiness to her son, and also to the young girl by her side.

Janet was speechless with amazement. Never had the faintest idea entered her head that Mr Darrel entertained any sentiments toward her other than those of friendship. She was quite as much astonished at Mrs Darrel's sanctioning this—at her speaking as she had done. If Mr Darrel did love her, she thought that his mother would endeavour to check any such feeling. Andrew—her father—a hundred thoughts flashed through her mind.

Mrs Darrel saw her agitation; she thought that she understood the cause of it. They had turned to go homewards.

"Did Mr Darrel know that you were going to speak to me?"

"No, I shall tell him when we return; tell him that you will not go on Monday."

"Don't, Mrs Darrel. Don't say a word to him."

"Janet, why not? Why deprive him of one hour's happiness? Remember his blindness, Janet."

"I *do* remember it, Mrs Darrel, I *do* remember it. That is why I wish you not to speak to him."

Mrs Darrel looked at her. She was a strange girl; *that* Mrs Darrel had always known; but her present conduct was incomprehensible. Janet Tudor was *not* the girl to affect coyness or coquetry. That Janet loved her son the mother did not for one moment doubt; she wished it, therefore she believed it. Was she not always happy to be with him, always seeking to amuse him, and to make him forget his blindness? Why did not Mrs Darrel look back to what had been the feelings of her own young heart? This unembarrassed intercourse argued friendship—surely not love.

They had nearly reached home. Mrs Darrel saw that Janet continued agitated; perhaps that was natural.

They were coming up the shrubbery path, that path up which Janet had led Mr Darrel years before.

"Now, Janet, you will let Edward speak to you himself?"

This was merely a polite form of speech; that Janet would refuse, Mrs Darrel did not at all suppose.

"No, Mrs Darrel—no, not now, I must think over all you have said; only, don't think me ungrateful."

Janet looked distressed. Mrs Darrel was vexed with her, yet she could not help feeling sorry for the young girl, standing alone as she did. And — she had not caught at a rich marriage, although it would take her from a life of toil. Difficulties in obtaining usually enhance the value of the desired object. Hitherto, all that Mrs Darrel had said and done, she had said and done merely because she thought it would bring happiness to her son; but when matters did not advance as rapidly as she had expected, the desire to overcome obstacles rose in her mind, and she became almost as impatient of delay as her son could have been. They had reached home. They had walked longer than they were aware of. It was close upon the dinner hour.

Janet was glad that there was no time for thought, before she must go down-stairs. She had scarcely time to take off her wraps, and wet boots, before the bell rang. As soon as she could, she ran down-stairs.

Mr Darrel was in the room; his mother crossed the hall a moment after herself. For once she felt the presence of those solemn-looking servants to be a comfort. The conversation at dinner was generally on indifferent subjects—to-day it was unusually constrained. There sat the three, making pretence to eat dinner for which they had no appetite. Janet talked about red lichens because she would not be conspicuously silent, but she scarcely knew what she said. The same subject was uppermost in each mind. Mr Darrel's face wore a gloomy expression; Janet did not look happy; Mrs Darrel sat at the head of her table, outwardly calm, but little nervous movements of her hands showed that she also was under excitement. Mr Darrel and his mother had their secret, and Janet and Mrs Darrel theirs; it was a comfort to Janet that *he* supposed her to be in ignorance of everything.

The ordeal of that dinner was over at last. Janet slipped away to her own room.

Mr Darrel and his mother were alone.

"Mother, what is the matter with Janet?"

Mrs Darrel was silent; she was a bad dissimulator.

"Mother, is anything the matter with Janet? Is she in any trouble?"

"No, not that I know of. What makes you think it?"

"Mother, don't try to deceive me, something *is* the matter. I know every tone of her voice, and perceive every change. Mother, you've been telling her what you found out this morning. Oh! why did you? Why did you? It is *that* which is troubling her. I *know* that she does not love me, never will love me, as *she* must love before she consents to become any man's wife. You don't know her, mother, you don't know the blessing she will be to the one she *can* love. We who are deprived of one faculty can sometimes understand more than you all."

He had grasped hold of the mantelpiece, and his whole frame shook.

"Edward, you think too little of yourself. Janet Tudor may consider herself a fortunate woman."

"Oh! mother! mother! *Can't* you understand? *She* won't think about being *fortunate*.

She'll marry where she loves, and nowhere else. If I was poor, she'd marry me if she loved me, and do the best she could for me. My position won't tempt her one bit."

Mrs Darrel had a better knowledge of Janet than would appear from her words; but she was indignant at the idea of her son's love meeting with no return.

"What should prevent her loving you?"

"Who knows? Is it not a mystery which none can interpret? Don't you remember what she was singing the other night?

'And tell me how love cometh?
'Tis here unseen, unsent;
And tell me how love goeth?
That was not *love* that went.'"

"Where is she?"

"Gone to her room; this has driven her away."

"Nonsense, Edward! I believe you will spoil her. She will come down presently. It's all very natural that she should wish to be alone. She was of course very much surprised. She never expected such good fortune."

"Mother, I *wish* you would not speak so."

They sat silently for a long time.

"Mother, what did she say?"

Mrs Darrel started; her thoughts had been wandering, not quite away from Janet and her son, but away from the present state of things.

He repeated,—"What did she say, mother?"

"Wished me not to tell you at present that I had spoken to her; said she must think of what I had told her."

"She did? God bless her!"

And Janet, when she reached her room, was so utterly amazed at the morning's revelation that she could think of nothing. By degrees she became more composed, and was able to think. Vaguely for a time she thought of her father, and Andrew, and Mr Darrel. It was a wonderful tale,—surely she must be dreaming,—Mrs Darrel, considered so proud, to sanction such a thing! Mr Bateman had rejected her. Mrs Darrel, who, the world would say, had more right to be proud, would take her to her heart as her son's wife.

Janet did not remember that her father had never injured Mrs Darrel, as he had injured Mr Bateman. Mrs Darrel saw her without prejudice, as she really was. Mr Bateman looked at her through a distorted medium, owing to his wrongs. Mrs Darrel would make a sacrifice of personal feeling to increase her son's happiness. Mr Bateman would inflict suffering rather than allow his son to entangle himself in a connection which he thought would bring him sorrow. Mrs Darrel's and Mr Bateman's actions were diametrically opposed, yet the influencing motive was the same. Then came *the* question,—What was she to do? Why had he loved her? Was it her fault? She threw herself on her bed, buried her eyes in the pillow, and held one corner so tight that all the blood seemed to have left her fingers. She had always thought of him as a very kind friend, nothing more; as such she esteemed him, loved him perhaps; yes, she did love him as such; she would do anything to help him, anything to amuse him, she liked being with him, but this was not love, not *the* love he sought, not the love which she ought to be capable of feeling, before she promised to be his wife, not the love which she would have felt for Andrew. Then there was his blindness, she was *so* sorry for him. Would he think that she could not love him on account of that? She must implore him not to think so. If anything *could* have made her love him, it would have been her pity for his blindness. She lay still for a little while, and then she rose, and walked up and down the room. After all, *need* she bring this disappointment upon him? She had loved Andrew. She knew that she should never again love any one as she had loved him, but she had heard nothing of him for a long time. No vows bound them. She might never see him again, or she might see him married to some one else; meet him how or when she would, his father would always be an obstacle to his marrying her. Mr Darrel loved her; he and his mother had been very kind friends to her. Why should she not show her gratitude by doing all in her power to make his life happy? A thousand little circumstances of ordinary occurrence bore a different interpretation now.

She remembered how happy he was when she read to him, and when she was learning new music, and when she drove him to Derwent. There is great happiness in making others happy, especially if that other person is deprived of some source of gratification which people generally possess. It was a pleasant picture to dwell on. For a few minutes she could easily have deluded herself into the idea that she loved him; and if Mrs Darrel had come into her room during those few minutes Janet would in all probability have gone down-stairs as Edward Darrel's future wife. As she stood there her eye rested on the book which Andrew had given her long before, and old remembrances came back so vividly that she could almost have believed that Andrew stood beside her. Then, what were her feelings as regarded Mr Darrel? Why, she thought, better a thousand times pain him now than wrong him by letting him think that a heart is entirely his when it is not. The old love was *not* dead; it never would be. As long as she remained unmarried it was no sin; but what if she should chance to meet Andrew when she was the wife of Edward Darrel? Why, she would be a good wife. But her heart quailed at the thought. She had no right to place such trial in her own way. She had no right to risk the happiness of three people. She had no right to marry Mr Darrel unless she could lay her hand on her heart and say that it was wholly and entirely his. Janet heaved one great sigh, and then she breathed more freely, as one escaped from a great danger. She must speak to Mrs Darrel, or write to her; that was no pleasant task—but it must be done, and the sooner done the better. She would write, it would be easier than speaking; she could put her letter on the table in Mrs Darrel's room. She took a sheet of paper and wrote, "Dear Mrs Darrel,"—then she came to a full stop. She sat thinking, How could she make Mrs Darrel understand without telling about Andrew? Tell that she could not. There had been a momentary gleam of happiness, and a great sorrow which was sacred; she could tell no one of that. After all, would it not be better to speak to Mrs Darrel? Black and white conveys none other than the literal meaning of the words;

in speaking you can soften or add additional force, as the case may seem to require it, by tone and manner. But the matter was decided for her. There was a knock at the door. Mrs Darrel entered.

Janet's heart beat fast. Quietly to say what you know will be unpleasant to the hearer requries a considerable amount of moral courage, and the difficulty is not diminished when the person whom you have to address is one for whom you have a regard, and to whom you are indebted for many acts of kindness. But there was no escape for Janet, even had she wished it; she *must* speak now, so she dashed at it. Her agitation made her feel choking, she should cry in another minute, she must not delay.

"I was just beginning to write to you, Mrs Darrel—I'd better go to-morrow—I'm so very much obliged to you and to Mr Darrel for your kindness to me—and—and—Oh! Mrs Darrel, I know you'll think me ungrateful, and I'm not, indeed I'm not. I'd do anything that was right to make you and Mr Darrel happy, but it would be wicked of me to marry him. I don't love him as his wife ought to love him, and I know that I never shall, and then he wouldn't be happy."

There, she had said it—now she must abide by the consequences. That was Janet's feeling.

For a moment Mrs Darrel was *very* angry. Her pride had received a wound, and a severe one. She had offered what had been rejected—rejected by one who had no pretensions to aspire to anything of the kind. She had sacrificed her feelings for nought. The happiness she had thought to secure for her son would never be his. She felt angry with the individual who deprived him of it. But she was a generous woman, and her anger quickly passed. Janet might be mistaken, but she acted as she believed to be right. And she thought that there were many girls she could name, more happily situated than was Janet, who would not have been scrupulous as to how great, or how little, their love might be, but would have caught at the chance of being Mrs Darrel of Eckington. More than ever she wished Janet to be her son's wife.

She went towards Janet, and laid her hand on her shoulder.

"Janet, you have not taken sufficient time to consider this; you must not give a hasty answer. You are none the less likely to be happy yourself, or to make my son a good wife, because you distrust yourself. Think it over again. If you would be more comfortable at Stoke we will send you there to-morrow, and we will fetch you again whenever you like."

Janet was greatly agitated.

"No, Mrs Darrel, thank you, I mustn't come back here. I'll go to-morrow, but I must stay there. I know you think me wrong, but I *am* doing right, indeed I am."

Mrs Darrel looked at her closely.

"Janet, do you love any one else? I have no right to ask you—it is for my son's sake."

Janet coloured crimson. "But," she faltered—"I shall never see him again."

Mrs Darrel left her, but it was in sorrow, not in anger. She went to her room, she could not go down-stairs and speak to her son immediately. She must tell him all; better he should know it at once than feed on a love which must be hopeless. For a little while she sat thinking how she could best break it to him. Suddenly she altered her purpose. She would *not* tell him at present, there was no occasion. That Janet *had* loved some one else she had been assured of by herself. She must have been very young, probably it was a boy-and-girl attachment, a childish fancy, with no real abiding love in it. Janet had said that she should never see this lover again. The feeling would die out, and then—Mrs Darrel was in real, downright earnest now, and no scheming mother ever contemplated securing a rich heiress for her son with more pleasure than Mrs Darrel did the possibility of seeing Janet her son's wife. Janet wished to return to Stoke the next day; perhaps it would make her more comfortable to do so, thought Mrs Darrel. The carriage should be ready to take her after breakfast. She hoped, nay, she felt assured, that it would not be long before Janet returned on a different footing. With this assurance she went down-stairs.

"Mother, you have been with *her?*"

"Yes, Edward, I have."

"Well?"

"Well, let everything rest for a time.

Say nothing to her. She wishes to return to Stoke to-morrow; perhaps it is better that she should, it is only two days before the time she intended going. I have told her that she shall have the carriage."

Mr Darrel sighed.

"She does not know," continued his mother, "that you know of my having spoken to her; better not let her know, it will make it easier for her, and to tell her would do you no good."

"Thank you, mother, for thinking of her."

The evening passed rather heavily. Janet remained up-stairs some time putting up her things, in readiness for her return on the next day. At last that was finished. She thought that she ought to go down-stairs. Mr Darrel was playing on his organ; she had heard a faint echo of the music when she was in her room; as she approached she recognized the "Qui Tollis" from Mozart's Twelfth Mass. She opened the door gently, and walked noiselessly across the room, so at least she thought, but he heard her.

"Sing me *one* song to-night, Janet."

She went towards the organ, she would much rather not sing, but she did not like to refuse.

He began playing "Adelaide."

"You haven't your music, Janet."

"I know it without."

Her few first notes were tremulous, but she sang it with feeling. When she had finished, Mr Darrel shut the organ, and felt his way to his old place beside the fire.

Janet was very thankful to hear the clock in the hall strike ten; it was the signal for the servants to come in to prayers. She had never before thought it possible that she should be glad to leave Mr and Mrs Darrel, yet so it was now.

CHAPTER III.

When Andrew Bateman heard that Janet was at Eckington, he took for granted that she was visiting Dr and Mrs Thorpe. For this reason she did not receive his letter; it was addressed to her at the Rectory; there the post-woman (for Eckington did not boast a post-man) left it, and Mr Selwyn's servant took it to Eckington Manor, just one hour after she had left.

Andrew's intention was to come and see her before she should have time to write and forbid his doing so.

About mid-day he was set down by one of the London coaches at the little lone road-side inn, which has before been mentioned. He had no need this time to inquire his way; but he walked through the snowy lanes towards the village, and went direct to the Rectory.

He inquired for Miss Tudor. The servant looked rather surprised, said that Miss Tudor was not there, but would he walk in? Master was at home.

Andrew was shown into the study; it was the same room in which he had seen Janet years before.

Mr Selwyn entered.

Andrew had expected to see his old master, Dr Thorpe. Here was a second disappointment.

There he learnt that Dr Thorpe and his wife were on the continent, and that Janet had been staying, not at the Rectory, but with Mrs Darrel.

"Is it far to Eckington Manor."

"No, my servant shall show you the way."

Andrew thought he could find his way alone.

"The shortest way from here is through my garden, and across the church-yard;

I will be your guide so far; after that you can scarcely go wrong."

Mr Selwyn put on his hat, and the two sallied forth through the garden and the little gate, by the same path by which Janet went the day she had first met Mr Darrel.

They reached the church-yard gate; from thence the chimneys of the house were visible.

"Now," said Mr Selwyn, "go a little way down the lane, and you will come to the gate, you cannot miss it."

Andrew thanked him, and went on his way.

Mr Selwyn stood a moment at the gate watching him. Brother, lover, friend, cousin? Which is he? Though the three last might be centred in one person. Men can be as curious as women sometimes. Not that Mr Selwyn had the slightest personal interest in the question. He admired Janet, and thought her a very nice girl, but without in the least failing in his allegiance to a certain lady whom he had asked to become Mrs Selwyn. Under any circumstances, he would not have wished to marry Janet, for she rather frightened him.

Andrew reached "The Manor." He again inquired for Miss Tudor; again was told that she was not there; and again was asked to walk in. Mrs Darrel was at home.

Mrs Darrel and her son were together.

"I was told at the Rectory that Miss Tudor was staying here; I find she has left."

"Yes, she left us this morning. You expected to find her at the Rectory?"

"Yes, I am an old pupil of Dr Thorpe's."

This, Andrew said by way of introduction, for Mrs Darrel was scanning him closely; then he added,—"I had hoped to see Dr Thorpe, but I find he is away from home."

"Yes, he has been absent more than six months."

The same queries as to who Andrew might be, and in what relation he might stand to Janet, which had made Mr Selwyn pause at the church-yard gate, came into Mrs Darrel's mind. He was not a brother, she was sure; in that case he would have spoken of Janet as his sister. However, the result of her scrutiny was satisfactory, as far as Andrew himself was concerned.

"Has Miss Tudor returned to 'The Vale?'" asked Andrew.

"No, she has not lived there for some time." He can't know much about her, thought Mrs Darrel. "Are you related to Miss Tudor?"

"No, but we're very old friends. Her brothers and myself were all pupils of Dr Thorpe, when he had the Grammar School at Holme."

Mrs Darrel felt quite sure that this must be the lover whom Janet had thought never to see again. That there was a history in the back-ground she nothing doubted; she longed intensely to know it.

Mr Darrel had not spoken; his face was so intelligent, and he had apparently *looked* at the speakers; Andrew had not perceived that he was blind. He felt that he *must* get Janet's present address. He was becoming more and more uneasy. She was evidently on very intimate terms here. He did her the justice to believe that external surroundings would not influence her, but he felt very jealous of Mr Darrel. He felt certain that they were rivals. He had neither heard of nor seen her for a long time. No promises bound her. This was the gentleman, no doubt, whom she had been seen driving in the little pony carriage. What a fool he was to imagine that it could be Dr Thorpe! All this passed rapidly through his mind. Then he asked Mrs Darrel in a very unconcerned manner, so he flattered himself, if she could give him Janet's address.

Mrs Darrel was more than ever confirmed in her suspicions. She did not at all wish to tell him where Janet was, yet she had no good reason for withholding the information from him. She gave him Janet's address, and he took his leave.

"Mother, did Janet ever tell you of any one who loved her?" said Mr Darrel when Andrew was gone.

"Why?"

"Why!—Why, because *he* loves her; and I thought she might have told you."

Now though the road from Eckington to Stoke was direct enough for Mrs Darrel, with her own carriage, it was circuitous for any one depending on public conveyances. Neither horse nor gig was to be hired at Eckington; walking seemed hopeless; the winter's day was drawing to a close; it was rapidly becoming dusk. Andrew had but a vague notion of the relative position of Stoke and Eckington, and the cross country lanes were some of them impassable from the snow.

The only course of proceeding was to retrace his steps as far as the little inn on the high road, to go by the next coach to Derwent, and to postpone his visit to Stoke to the following day.

As there was no choice, nothing on which to decide, there was nothing to prevent his setting out at once. He looked at his watch, it was nearly four, he thought there must be a coach passing about that time. He walked quickly on. As he approached the end of the lane he heard the sound of wheels and the trampling of horses along the hard, frosty high road. It must be a coach. He quickened his steps. The sound of wheels and trampling of feet had ceased, but there were voices to be heard. Andrew ran the rest of the way down the lane; there was the coach standing before the inn. It was beginning to sleet hard.

"Full outside, plenty of room inside," said the coachman, opening the coach door.

Andrew got in.

By the side of the coach was standing a vehicle, to what species it belonged is unknown, but its owner called it a "trap." The occupants of the trap were in the inn, from whence they emerged when the coachman inquired "if they was a-going on?" The woman got into the coach, in company with a band-box, tied up in a blue cotton pocket-handkerchief, a large bag worked in variegated cruels, and a red and green worsted comforter.

"We was fortunate to get in afore the snow comed down!" said the owner of the comforter.

Andrew assented.

"They makes the coaches most uncomfortable small!"

Andrew suggested that there would have been more room if she had given the band-box in charge of the coachman. It was an unfortunate remark, for it opened the flood-gates of the woman's eloquence.

"No, sir, I couldn't no ways trust it to the coachman, which isn't careful as he ought to be, considerin' how expensive travellin' is, not to say that he always expec's somethin' for hisself. I had the genteelest bonnet spiled by this *very* coach, sir; which was a pink silk with a green feather, which I wore to my poor sister's weddin', which is dead an' gone, leavin' six children, an' four on 'em has the measles."

The speaker paused, and wiped her eyes, whether at the thought of the deceased sister, the spoiled bonnet, or the measles, is unknown.

"I'm goin' to see my other sister, 'tis an out-of-the-way place where she lives; they knows nothin' about the fashions, so as Holme is, as you may say, a place where you may get anything, I thought I might so well bring her a bonnet, which is the reason I wouldn't give the box to the coachman, and hoping it don't ill-convenience you, sir!"

As Andrew did not reply, the woman found talking dull, and therefore sought other amusement. From the depths of the worked bag she produced a large paper of sandwiches; but these were not arrived at without first dislodging a pair of slippers, a hair-brush, a paper of peppermint lozenges, and a box of hair-pins.

The woman offered Andrew some of the sandwiches, and when he refused she pressed him to partake of them.

She again dived into the worked bag, and produced a medicine bottle, containing something stronger than wine, and a wine glass with a broken stem. After partaking freely of the contents of the medicine bottle she fell asleep.

There was another inside passenger, a tall thin man, past middle age, with a delicately-formed nose and high, narrow forehead; it was a face which indicated taste and culture rather than talent; possibly taste might, from weakness of character, have degenerated into fastidiousness, which made it a torment rather than a pleasure to the possessor.

This third passenger was habited in the most approved of travelling wraps; a pair of dark sable cuffs guarded his wrists from the cold wind, and he was almost covered up by a seal-skin rug. The objects of his care and devotion appeared to be a very small and tightly done-up brown silk umbrella, which reposed on the vacant seat beside Andrew, and a glossy and well-brushed hat, which he had hung up in the roof of the coach, having put on a grey travelling cap.

The tall man did not speak. He regarded Andrew with a look of commiseration, as he sat opposite the talkative woman with her horrid band-box obtruding itself on to his knees. When the sandwiches and the medicine bottle were produced, he shrank back into his corner in intense disgust. His pity for Andrew soon went, or was turned into contempt. He had thought him a gentleman; he must have been mistaken, for there he sat, unmoved, while that horrid woman satisfied her voracious appetite, and—and—then—snored!

But they were not to reach Derwent without the fourth seat being occupied. The sleet turned into rain; every object looked drenched. The coach pulled up where four roads met. A man carrying a box, and a fat woman in pattens, stood by the road-side. The box was deposited under the tarpaulin. The coach door opened; the fat woman, cloak, shawls, pattens, all got in. She knocked her large wet bonnet against the tall man's hat, and flattened it, and was just sitting down on the slender brown silk umbrella, when Andrew rescued it and placed it in the corner by his side. The tall man took down his hat, pushed it into shape, and tenderly smoothed it, his face indicating great suffering. There was no escape, he shrank as far as possible back into his corner. The wet fat woman with the pattens sat in front, and appropriated much more than a fourth part of the inside of the coach, and the woman with the medicine bottle and sandwiches sat by his side; there were crumbs from the sandwiches lying on his rug. Further and further he retreated, until it was impossible to compress himself into a smaller space. He was no further from the causes of his annoyance; every inch he gave they took, and thought what a particularly accommodating gentleman he was.

The coach rolled on through rain and mud; it was a dreary ride. The woman with the sandwiches was asleep, and dreamed of the baby faces whose little hands would be busy turning out aunty's bag at her journey's end, to see what she had brought them. The fat farmer's wife was wondering what sort of a place she should find London, after all, bigger perhaps than two or three Derwents put together, and hoping that her poor sick son would be no worse before she could reach him, and that the fresh eggs she had taken with her would arrive safely. And the tall man, shrinking from his fellow-creatures, was pitying himself; thinking how much a man of taste and refinement, such as himself, had to put up with if he travelled by a public conveyance. He thought of his rooms in St Werburgh's, no jostling against the common herd there. The fellows of St Werburgh's would be sitting, after Hall, sipping their wine; the chapel bell would be ringing, it was a surplice night, there would be an anthem; the tall man liked good music, and the music at St Werburgh's *was* good. Here was he, in a dirty coach, with dirty people, suffering martyrdom. He would give his servant instructions to fumigate his great-coat and rug, and long should it be ere he again quitted the decorous precinct of St Werburgh's.

Andrew was thinking how he should proceed on his journey to Stoke. The London coach went no further in that direction than Derwent.

"Can you tell me whether there is a coach from Derwent to Stoke?" Andrew addressed the tall man.

"Sir, I am a stranger, and know nothing of this part."

His tone and manner conveyed the idea that he thought it a great impertinence to address him without previous introduction, also that he felt no interest in the affairs of ordinary people.

Andrew said no more. He could get what information he required at the inn at Derwent.

The tall man suddenly perceived that Andrew had taken care of his cherished umbrella. He stretched out his hand to take it to himself, and was profuse in thanks, and elaborate apologies for the inconvenience it might have occasioned.

The dreary ride for Andrew was at an end. The coach had reached Derwent. It stopped at the inn to change horses, and Andrew got out.

After a wet, cold journey there is something very consolatory in the large blazing fire at an inn, and the little table drawn up by the side with the cloth laid ready for dinner. Andrew felt it when he emerged from the coach, cramped and cold, on that dreary evening. Creature comforts, people of the Quaker persuasion would call them, and none are better purveyors, as well as appreciators, of the same than those patrons of broad brims.

There are hard, strong-minded people in the world, who think it, if not a sin, at any rate a weakness, to regard these things.

Better plead guilty to the weakness than own the strong, hard mind.

A vexatious occurrence, thought over, after a long cold ride, on a dismal winter day, seems a mountain; the same occurrence canvassed two hours later, when you are in dry clothes, by a warm, bright fire, and after a good dinner, if it does not actually dwindle to a molehill, does not present its annoyances in such gigantic proportions.

Andrew had felt drowsy when sitting by the fire; no sooner had he gone to bed than all disposition to sleep left him. He had had no time to think during the day; now thought became active enough. His interview with the Darrels came before him. He had from the first experienced a vague feeling of suspicion that Mr Darrel was a rival. The house became more and more quiet, the footsteps along the passages less and less frequent; at last all seemed to have retired for the night. The quieter the house the more active became Andrew's thoughts. The possibility of Mr Darrel being a rival became a probability, and finally a certainty. With the certainty came the question of the extent of Janet's love for himself. Would it be proof against all which Mr Darrel could offer her? One minute he did her justice, and believed it would; the next he magnified tenfold the advantages of Mr Darrel's position, repeated to himself that Janet was bound by no promises, that his own father was the obstacle to his marrying her. He had a suspicion that his father had been rude to her. In the face of all this, would she refuse Mr Darrel? His heart sank. With his exaggerated notions, exaggerated in the silence of the night, of all that Mr Darrel could offer, came a corresponding mistrust of himself, and a sense of his own deficiencies, some of which scarcely existed, but thought created or magnified them to torment him. Sleep *would* not come; he twisted and turned, heard clock after clock strike the different hours, heard the mail drive up and somebody called to go by it; the night seemed interminable. At last he fell asleep, and dreamed of Janet, and Mr Darrel, and his fellow-passengers of the previous day—that they had all conspired against him, and had entangled him in a most intricate plot, and that some one was shouting at him. He woke, and found that the servant had brought his hot water, and had been knocking at the door for ten minutes, trying to make him hear.

CHAPTER IV.

The rain had gone. The morning was bright and frosty, and exhilarating. The coach ran lightly along the frozen ground, and the horses tossed up their heads and snorted, as though theirs was not work that day, but play.

Andrew had shaken off some of his gloomy forebodings. It is in the silence of the night that thought runs riot, and takes possession like a demon. When the morning comes, with calls for physical exertion, and bringing outer world objects to claim attention, the demon is obliged to abdicate. Vexed questions *will* arise, which time alone can decide. Positions of difficulty, in which you are powerless to move, and which time alone can change. Such things *will* happen while we are dwellers upon earth. You sit still, and why not, since you can do nothing? and thought comes and mocks you like a fiend. Don't sit still; if thinking can do you no good, dethrone thought. Patiently wait and trust, but don't wait in inactivity; *that* is giving the demon full power over you. Apart from that trust which is the good man's strength—and it need not be opposed to it, but may go hand in hand with it—an active practical life is the best antidote for the trials of life, gives the greatest power to fight against them, rather, it is in itself a great power before which they bow. So, if a trouble has overtaken you which you can neither lessen nor avert, find something to do. Most people *have* something to do, something which they *ought* to do. Do it, the trouble will seem less; neglect it, the trouble will increase in proportion to the duty neglected. If you really have nothing to do, make something. Go into your poor neighbour's cottage, and learn how she and her husband and seven children live on nine shillings a week, and she has to wash, and make, and mend, and cook for them all, and she has her own heart-troubles as well as you, then come home and try to do something to help her, something which shall make her heart glad; see then if your own troubles won't seem lighter. Do something. If you can find nothing else to do, take a long walk, in spite of wind and weather, but don't sit and brood over trouble with folded hands, making it an excuse for idleness. To do so is to abdicate in favour of a demon, and a demon very difficult to dethrone when once he has taken possession.

Andrew had reached the nearest point to Stoke which the coach passed, and was set down near a sign-post on the common. After walking for a short time he saw Stoke before him. It looked a nest of poor cottages. What could Janet do in such a place as that?

He took out of his pocket-book a card, on which he had written Janet's address. Mrs Darrel had told him that Farmer Harris lived quite the other side of the village.

He passed the little church and schoolhouse; the school had not yet opened. One or two women and children looked out of their cottage doors after him; it was so seldom that the Stoke people saw strangers.

He reached the gate of a small farm. This must be the place, but he thought it a strange home for Janet. Why was she there?

He went through the farm-yard, and knocked at the door. A voice, which he recognized as Grace's, said, "Come in."

"Bless me! If it isn't Mr Andrew."

There was a work-box on the little table by the fire, and a small silver thimble, which did not look as though it belonged either to the farmer's wife or to Grace; and by the box was the drawing-book which Andrew had given Janet years before—he noticed it all.

"Is Miss Tudor here?"

"Yes, Mr Andrew, I'll call her. I take it she'll be right glad to see you, as I be. She only came from Mrs Darrel's yesterday."

Grace left the room. Andrew heard her say, "Miss Janet, there's some one wants to see you down-stairs."

"Who is it?" asked Janet, "I'm very busy."

"Never mind that, 'tis some one as you'll be glad to see."

She came down.

"Andrew!"

"Yes, Janet. Are you not glad to see me?"

Her face said she was glad.

"I've found you out at last."

Janet looked up inquiringly.

"I've gone towards 'The Vale' often, hoping to meet you, until I felt sure that you could not be there. Then I heard, by chance, that you were staying at Eckington; of course I thought you were visiting the Thorpes. I wrote and told you that I was coming, which letter I suppose you have not received. Well, I went to Eckington, and found neither you nor the Thorpes, but heard that you were visiting Mrs Darrel. I went there to find that you had just left; but she gave me your address, and I followed you here."

Now Janet, as a very discreet young lady, and in accordance with her own expressed determination to do nothing without Mr Bateman's approval, ought of course to have inquired of Andrew if he had his father's sanction for coming, and, as he had not, she ought to have sent him away without speaking another word..

But she did not. Instead of acting like a discreet young lady, whose heart, supposing her to possess any, is well under control, Janet made the wood-fire burn up brightly, and told Andrew that she was very glad to see him.

Then they remained silent. Janet felt too happy to speak, and too thankful that no feeling of pity or gratitude had made her accept Mr Darrel. For a little while she forgot all the sorrow which this love-tale had brought her.

Andrew's misgivings were set at rest by Janet's bright face. But everything was so strange. Why was she there? What had happened? A thousand questions came crowding into his mind; a thousand things which he wanted to know; yet he sat silent, only feeling how happy he was to be there. But this must not last; he must speak.

"How long since you were at 'The Vale,' Janet?"

"I've not been there for more than a year. I don't live there now, you know."

"Why not?"

"It's a long story, the why not—I *couldn't* stay there, Andrew; I dare say many people would call me foolish, but I couldn't."

"*I* should not call you foolish. I'm sure you've not done anything wrong. Tell me about it."

There was a pained expression on Janet's face, as though an old sorrow was revived.

"I dare say I was hasty, but I did nothing really wrong. I can't tell it all over again; but you'll understand. I *couldn't* stop to hear those I love best reviled." Then she added in a low voice, "There may have been great faults, I don't deny that, but they needn't have told *me* of them."

Andrew could not understand how she should be there, how she lived, what she could be doing.

Janet's gladness at seeing him passed away. There was a barrier between them when she lived at "The Vale;" would it not be greater than ever now!

"Do your uncles and aunts like your being here?"

"No, but I'm not sorry I came, I should do the same again."

He had to drag out everything which he wanted to know. To tell him of a life of drudgery would be to strengthen feelings in his heart which would bring them both sorrow—so she felt. Pride said too—His father shan't say that I've made out a pitiful case to work on his son's heart.

"Do they come and see you?"

"Who? My uncles and aunts? They did not for some time. They were not pleased that I would not come back and live at 'The Vale.' Uncle Jeremiah promised that everything should be different. I dare say he meant what he said, but he was offering what he had no power to carry out. It might have been better for a little time, and then it would have been just the same as before."

"So they gave you up?"

"For some time they did, all except Uncle Esau; he was always kind. He came to see me, and told me to let him know if I wanted anything. I never *have* wanted anything, and I'm glad I haven't. Not that I should mind accepting anything from him, he doesn't make one feel like a pauper receiving alms; still it's best and pleasantest to trust to one's self.

What *could* she be doing, thought Andrew, in that retired place? But he did not like to ask the question direct. Janet was speaking like her old self. *She* a pauper receiving alms! She didn't look like one. He laughed at the thought.

"Did they make you feel that?"

"Aunt Wood tried to; but I was going to tell you, Uncle Esau was always kind. Aunt Mary was away, therefore knew nothing about my going. It is Aunt Wood who is mistress, and it is she therefore who can make you comfortable or uncomfortable. She rules even Uncle Jeremiah in some things."

Janet continued, "Grace told me that Uncle Jeremiah and Aunt Mary came here to see me a few days after I had gone to

Eckington. They wrote to me when I was there, and Uncle Jeremiah sent me a present, I can't think what made him do it."

Andrew thought that Jeremiah Higgins' generosity was caused by Janet's being a visitor in a grand house, but he did not say so. What *could* she be doing at Stoke?

"So you live with Grace—I saw her as I came in."

"Grace was living here, the Harrises are relations of hers, they could take me in too, and I'm very comfortable, more comfortable than I should be in most places; between Grace and Mr Harris, I'm well taken care of."

Andrew took up the drawing-book, which he had given her, from the table; it looked well used, and there were marginal notes in pencil.

"You have studied this a great deal. Do you draw much?"

"I haven't much time."

He looked surprised; what could she have to do in that place?

She answered the look.

"You think I have nothing to do here; of course you don't know how I'm circumstanced. Mr Platt wanted a mistress for his school. I wanted employment by which I could earn something. He rather objected to me at first—I suppose he did not think me old or steady enough; however, he was willing to try me, and I've continued here ever since. I've had the school a year. When the organist left I took his place. You don't know what an important person I'm become!"

But Andrew *did* know that, however gaily she might speak, he had heard of a life of toil, and that she could have but a pittance to depend on.

"Oh, Janet! What a life for you! What hard work!"

"Hard work! That's as people think. I don't know that it's harder than many other kinds of work. As to the organ, I'm very fond of music. You pity me because I'm *obliged* to do it. Everybody is obliged. If I had a fortune left me, that would not exempt me from work, unless I was ill or disabled. You should see Mrs Darrel, with her steward, and her farmers, and her leases and account-books, and poor people,—she's rich, but she isn't idle. Mr

Darrel *can't* do all this, because he's blind, it isn't required of him. But every able-bodied person has some duty which their station requires them to perform, and if they think that riches free them from the necessity of exertion, they are mistaken. None of your miserable, helpless, vapid creatures for me, a trouble to themselves and to every one else!"

She spoke bravely, and certainly did not look like a toil-worn woman, fighting the "battle of life." She made light of her daily life. Andrew of all people must not know of the struggle.

Andrew was not deceived. He understood her present mood. If ever he felt hardly towards his fellow-man, it was then. Why would his father cling to those narrow, preconceived notions of Janet's character? Miserable folly! If old age is wary, it need not be suspicious! Without putting his love into the scale, he would do better to marry Janet penniless than many women with a fortune. Then there were the Tudors, Janet's nearest relations, a father and two sons, hale and strong, and yet to let her toil and toil for a pittance! If hard thoughts could really take effect, the Tudors' position at that moment would have been unpleasant. And if Janet had known what was passing in his mind, she would have said, "Nay, Andrew, I have no wish to be a burden on my brothers; they have their way to make, I can do for myself."

"It's all very well, this work, while you're strong and well, but you may be ill and unable to do it, Janet."

"Every one is liable to contingencies."

"But what would you do?"

"I've saved some money." She hoped not to spend it over herself though.

What *would* he hear next? he thought.

She continued. "But this seemed the right thing, perhaps the *only* thing, for me to do; so I'm doing it. I don't trouble much about the future now. 'Man proposes'—you know the rest. Don't discourage me, though."

There was a tinge of sadness in her voice; probably she herself was not aware of it, but Andrew detected it.

"Janet, Janet, don't say that this

miserable work is the only thing you can do! It's not, and you *know* that it's not. No, you don't know all, you don't know that I can offer you a home, though it may be but an humble one."

For one moment she was deceived. On another occasion he had said, "If my father should consent, but if he should leave me nothing, would you have me then?" and she had said "Yes." Had this come to pass?

But she saw her mistake.

"Andrew, if you gained a wife you would lose your father, and *I* should be the cause of the estrangement."

"He would get over it when he knew you."

"Possibly, but I don't think he would. If he despised me then, he will despise me more now. He will think, and the world will confirm him in his opinion, that the village school-mistress is still less fit to be his son's wife than Miss Tudor, living at 'The Vale,' and ranking at any rate among respectable people."

She spoke very proudly.

Andrew had no petty pride himself. He

would not in the least have cared if all the world had known her position. He said,

"Under my roof none would dare to despise you."

"They would not dare show it, you mean. Probably not. They would gloss it over with extra politeness, and make me feel it the more. Andrew, I've had some experience of the world's ways in these things. I know that I've stepped down from the pedestal of gentility, and must abide by what I've done, or have been obliged to do. I'm not ashamed of it. I'm looked upon as a village school-mistress, which I am; I claim attention as nothing more. I always get my due share of respect as the school-mistress. Some treat me as a lady, so much the better for me when they do, but I don't exact it, and don't trouble myself about it. I'm able to earn enough to supply my wants, thank God, and I have something over. I'm proud, I know it, I don't mind working, I don't mind people's saying *now*, 'She's only a school-mistress,' but I *should* mind being patronized, and looked down on, if I was your wife, and you'd mind it too, and it would make us both miserable."

He knew that she was proud, but was hardly prepared for her pride being an obstacle to the attainment of his wishes. He thought, how little his father understood her.

"But, Janet, are you not fancying what might never come to pass? You have been Mrs Darrel's guest. I suppose *she* did not despise you?"

"No, of course not, or I should not have gone there. I have received very great kindness from Mrs Darrel, but every one is not like her."

Janet felt her colour rise at mention of Mrs Darrel. She would have given a great deal to have prevented it, but she could not, she knew that she was crimson to the very ends of her fingers.

Andrew noticed it. He remembered that Mrs Darrel had a son. His jealousy had disappeared when he saw Janet; now it returned.

"And Mr Darrel was as kind as his mother probably?" He said it in such a cold sneering tone.

Janet looked up, but merely answered, "Yes, they were both very kind to me, as kind as could be."

Andrew was standing by the open chimney; he kicked a piece of wood impatiently into the fire, and then turned abruptly round until he faced Janet.

"Janet," he said, and his voice was husky, "was there never a word of love spoken between you?"

She might have said, "Never." Mr Darrel had never spoken; but she felt that it would be a deception.

"Andrew, that's a question you have no right to ask."

"No right! It may be, yet I ask it."

He looked almost as though his life hung on her answer.

"He has been a kind friend ever since I was a child, Andrew. I've known him almost as long as I've known you; but there's nothing more."

"Can you lay your hand on your heart, and say, 'There never has been?'"

"Oh! Andrew, indeed you ought not to question me. It is not generous."

"Generous! What on earth has come to you? You are full of strange notions!"

She was silent. What *could* she say? She wished no one to know what had passed at Eckington, yet Andrew was vexed and unhappy.

"Janet," he said more gently, "if it had not been for untoward circumstances you would have been my wife long before this time. I should have had a husband's power to protect you, a husband's right to question you, though God grant I might never abuse it. That this is not the case is my misfortune, not my fault. Is it strange, therefore, that I should wish to know all that concerns you? Tell me, Janet, I *don't* think you love Mr Darrel, but I *do* think that he loves you."

She remained silent.

"Janet!"

"He never told me of his love, but his mother did."

"And wished you to marry him."

"Yes."

"And you refused."

"Yes."

"And in consequence have lost their friendship."

"No, I think not."

"Why did you refuse Mr Darrel, if you are going to let my father be an eternal barrier between yourself and me? Mr Darrel could offer you a home such as I have no pretensions to. He appears to be a gentleman, and his love must have been sincere."

"How *dare* you talk to me about a home such as you have no pretensions to? How *dare* you suppose I would be bribed by a fine house? What have I done that you should insult me like that? I refused Mr Darrel because I didn't love him. He and his mother have been kind friends to me, some of the kindest and best I ever had. I'm very sorry that he should have loved me. I know that he's unhappy, and that I am the cause of it, but it's not my fault; I must bear it, so must he. I won't wrong either him or myself by marrying one man while I love another."

She had been very angry when she began speaking; towards the end her manner softened.

"Andrew, now let this subject drop for ever. I did not wish any one to know it. You must keep the secret, and do as you would be done by."

This was the girl, thought Andrew, whom his father considered mercenary and scheming. He had come, hoping to overrule her objections; he saw that that would be impossible for the present. Disappointed though he might be, he felt more than ever confident of her truth and love. Would nothing induce his father to do her justice?

The winter's day was closing, Andrew must go. He lingered on, but he must go, he must leave her.

"God bless you, Janet!" He kissed her.

She stood watching him, as he went across the yard, and down the road, until he was lost behind the trees. She was glad to have seen him, glad to have heard the sound of his voice. It seemed an assurance of her having done right in refusing Mr Darrel. Her heart did not sink, as it used to do at these partings. Perhaps because she was more self-reliant.

Perhaps because after one crushing sorrow, nothing is ever again felt so keenly. Perhaps because she had learnt to accept pleasures when they came, and to be thankful for them, but not to expect them to continue always.

CHAPTER V.

Tom Tudor's student life had come to a close. It had been a pleasant life to him. He had gained considerable applause without hard work, rather, perhaps, without work which was disagreeable to himself. When a subject was fresh, and consequently interesting to him, he could show a considerable amount of energy; would study it eagerly, and leave plodding men far behind. His student life had been very pleasant; he had made pleasant acquaintances; now, just as he was beginning to tire of it all, a change came of itself, naturally, and without his seeking it. So it had been with him hitherto through life; everything had happened according to his taste. When he was getting tired of the routine of the old Holme grammar-school Dr Thorpe went to Eckington, and he accompanied him, and though the old books went too, yet the circumstances under which he studied them were so changed that everything appeared under a novel aspect; when the novelty of his life at Eckington had worn off, he entered on another phase of life, as a medical student; and when he began to weary of this again, a change was in store for him.

Uncle Jeremiah had been displeased with Tom. Tom had no business to be spending his money, lounging at fashionable watering-places; money was given him to pay the expenses of a student's life, not the life of a man of pleasure. When Tom took no notice of Uncle Jeremiah's letter of remonstrance, Uncle Jeremiah was still more wrath. Aunt Wood poured oil on the flame. Uncle Jeremiah said that such conduct was adding insult to injury. Aunt Wood added, "As was the custom of those Tudors to do, she'd no patience with 'em, nor with them as threw away their money on 'em." Now Uncle Jeremiah had resolved to have nothing more to do with Tom, and if Aunt Wood had said nothing, probably he would have adhered to his resolution; but ever since Janet's departure Uncle Jeremiah had been very restive when his eldest sister made acrimonious remarks; formerly he used to obey her, now he often made a point of going in a contrary direction. There were other reasons also why Uncle Jeremiah made up his mind to pocket the affront, and not to cast his nephew off; unless some one advanced a little money to enable Tom to set up in practice for himself, all that had hitherto been expended would have been thrown away.. Flattering accounts of Tom's talent continued to reach Uncle Jeremiah from time to time, until he began to think his nephew would be *the* genius of the age. These reasons, with the determination not to be governed by Aunt Wood, made him say to himself that Tom should not be prevented setting up for want of a little more money.

Uncle Jeremiah would like to see him established in some little country town. In a large place he might for a time be lost in the crowd, but in a small town he would immediately become a star of some magnitude, from the very day when the red lamp blazed over his door. But this did not at all coincide with Tom's views. He had been accustomed to good society, and Tom's interpretation of good society was not determined by money or position, although he despised neither, but his good society meant people who had minds and who used them, and who had qualifications, either natural or acquired, for being pleasant companions. "A small country town!" said Tom to himself. "Good God! what *is* Jeremiah Higgins thinking of? A small country town! A doctor—that would be myself,—a parson, a lawyer, and some nondescripts, expected to go to a tea-party once a week, heavy men, ill-dressed Misses, sipping tea, and saying Yes and No. None of that for me!" Tom did not give these reasons to Uncle Jeremiah for not wishing to settle in a small country town; he suggested whether there would be sufficient scope for him, and said that he should prefer the metropolis. Uncle Jeremiah had nothing to object. An opening was found, and Tom was set up in the corner of a certain square, with the orthodox red lamp over his door, and a conspicuous brass plate with T. Tudor, and a number of letters after his name, on it. Tom liked his new life exceedingly at first; success seemed to follow him here, as it had done elsewhere; plodding men might strive and strive, and woo the fickle goddess, to Tom Tudor she came unsought. At first he liked his uncertain, unsettled life, never knowing when he might be called out; he was interested in watching human nature under its various aspects, amused with the strange perversities and crotchets which he encountered, and he got a glimpse into secret histories, and romances of private life, which would have been a valuable stock in trade if he had turned author. About his profession itself he cared not in the least; the novelty soon wore off; he found it an intolerable nuisance to be at everybody's beck and call, to be summonsed from pleasant friends to minister to some cross old crotchety woman, who had not much the matter with her, and who might just as well have delayed sending for him until the next morning. Tom had numerous friends in London, as he had had in Edinburgh, and he was constantly with them; people thought at first that it was his professional engagements which took him so much from home; they said, "Dear me, what a practice that young man has!" Another medical man set up close by, and Tom's business decreased; at the same time he discovered that a surgeon's practice involved a great deal that was disagreeable to him; he thought also that it was very hard work in proportion to the pay, and that it would suit him much better to become an M.D. Uncle Jeremiah was rather pleased when he heard of this; he thought "Dr Tudor" sounded very respectable; his only misgiving was that money was always going out, and never coming in; and Tom was always *going* to do this and the other, but never did it. Where distinction was merely honorary Tom had been successful; but now that he was in the real practical world he let everything slip past him. Aunt Wood hit the truth, and if she had been less disagreeable she might have done some good; she said

"Tom's clever enough, but he's idle, he don't like work, only pleasure; he'd have had a good practice, as 'ud have paid him well, if he'd stuck to it like young Mr Smith." She was right, but she said it spitefully, and Uncle Jeremiah told her that she knew nothing about it; and Tom became in due time an M.D., much to his own satisfaction.

Janet was plodding on with her school-work. It was a cold spring, trying alike to the children and to her, and she was looking forward to her few days' holiday at Easter. It is only those who have to follow one routine, and that rather a weary one, day after day, punctual to certain hours, who know the intense relief of the short respite, the feeling in the morning I may spend to-day as I like, and apportion the hours as best suits me.

Janet returned from the school one afternoon.

"There's a letter for you, Miss Janet," said Grace. "The post were late this morning, an' it comed after you were gone."

"Where is it?" Janet was eager after

letters. She had not heard for some time from her father.

Grace took it down from the high chimney-piece, where she had put it under a brass candlestick to keep it safe.

Janet tore it open. It was in a strange hand-writing. It was no letter, only two cards tied together with a silver thread. Mr Harry Tudor was on one, Mrs Harry Tudor on the other.

Janet was so much surprised that she said nothing, but stood still, in the middle of the kitchen, twirling round the cards by the silver thread.

"Well, Miss Janet!" said Grace.

"Here, Grace." Janet held out the cards.

Grace was by no means a proficient either in reading or writing; it took her some time to understand the cards. After some spelling and repetition she made out "Mr Harry Tudor." "That's Master Harry," said Grace. After awhile "Mrs Harry Tudor" was splendid out. "Why, he's married! bless him! Mrs Harry *must* be his wife, Miss Janet." Grace had not been at all pleased with Harry, displeased that he did not take more notice of his sister, but he was one of her nurslings, and she could not help saying "God bless him!" when she heard of his being married. When she began to think of it her displeasure returned again. Why was not Janet at the wedding? She ought to have been.

"Who is she, Miss Janet? Who is it he's married?"

It was the question Janet had been asking herself. The only person she could think of was one of the Misses Saunders, but after all she did not fancy that *she* was Mrs Harry Tudor. She took the cards from Grace, and went up-stairs to take off her bonnet. She was too much surprised to feel hurt that Harry had not asked her to his wedding.

CHAPTER VI.

"I WONDER they isn't afraid o' breaking their necks!" Grace said this; she was standing at the door watching a very high dog-cart with red wheels, which was coming along the road.

"You see, Grace, it don't seem as high to them as is used to it;" having said this, John Harris went across the yard to look after his pigs.

The high dog-cart stopped at the gate. The driver called to a boy who was in the yard to come and hold the horse, and then jumped out and went towards the house.

Grace's curiosity had been highly excited, and her neck stretched forward as far as possible, in her endeavours to ascertain who the visitor might be.

"Bless us! if it ain't Master Harry." Grace met him at the door. "Walk in, Master Harry, an' I hope you're well, sir, an' Mrs Harry likewise, though, for the matter o' that, I think you *might* have asked your sister to your wedding, or leastways have told her who the lady were!"

Harry followed Grace into the kitchen without knowing what to say; it was not his custom to submit to be called to account by any one; but before Grace he felt much as he used to do in his school-boy days, when they lived in the old house at Holme, and when she rebuked him for any misdemeanour.

"I'm glad to see you, Master Harry, though I 'spose I should say Mr Harry now, seeing you're married, but you might have asked your sister to your wedding, an' not been married in this unbeknown way, as though you was ashamed of your wife, or your sister, or both."

"Where's Janet? I thought she would be here about this time."

"No, she don't often come home until

a'ter the a'ternoon school, but I'll send for her." Grace went out into the yard; the only person to be seen was the boy who was holding the horse.

"Run down to the school an' tell Miss Tudor to come here as quick as she can, 'cause there's some one as wants to see her; an' if she shouldn't be at the school, see if she's in the church, mind you find her."

"I'm minding the gen'leman's horse," said the boy.

"Never mind, do as I tell you, run off this minit. I'll see the horse don't come to no harm."

The boy did as Grace desired. Grace went back into the kitchen. "Master Harry, couldn't you put your horse into the stable? I've sent the boy to tell Miss Janet, an' the man's gone to Derwent, an' I don't know where John Harris is gone to; he was here not a minit ago, but people is always out o' the way jist when they's wanted."

The horse was put into the stable, and Harry went back into the kitchen to wait for Janet. Grace saw her coming up the road, and went to the gate to meet her.

"Master Harry's in the kitchen, that's why I sent for you. Why, how fast you've walked, you're quite out of breath!"

"And his wife. Is his wife with him?"

"No, only hisself."

Harry turned round as his sister entered the kitchen.

"Well, Harry!"

"Well, Janet!"

For a minute they stood by the fire, and said not a word more. Both were thinking of Harry's marriage. Harry felt awkward because he had not told his sister of it before, and Grace's words had not made him more comfortable.

"You had cards from us two or three weeks ago?"

"Yes, and was so surprised."

"I thought you would be. You see one can't ask everybody to one's wedding, and if you ask some and not others people take offence. Lucy's got a lot of cousins; she'd liked to have asked some, but she couldn't choose without offending the rest, so she asked none."

Janet did not see the parallel between Mrs Harry Tudor's numerous cousins and

Harry's only sister, but she did not say so; it was a long time since she had seen any of her own family, and sometimes her heart yearned after the familiar faces who had been her companions in childhood; she did not wish to say anything which might seem unkind to Harry, now that he had come to see her. She had been surprised to hear that he was married, but not surprised that he had not asked her.

"Lucy wants to know you, Janet; she wanted to come with me, but the day was too cold, I told her."

The day *was* cold, very cold; but if it had been mild and sunny Harry Tudor would not have brought his wife to see Janet, in her old school dress, at John Harris's.

"Lucy! I thought you liked Carry Saunders."

Harry coloured a little. "And you were taken in by a little civility, were you? You're as green as ever in some things. We can't marry every pretty girl we're civil to, and you wouldn't have us rude, would you?"

"No, but I thought you were something more than civil."

"I don't suppose Carry thought so, *she* knew what she was about."

"Well, I hope so, but—"

"Never mind any 'buts,' she's an arrant little flirt. You don't understand the world, Janet, and never will. Men often make girls believe themselves angels, and all the while they think them fools."

"Then it's very dishonourable of you, and very heartless, and very cruel."

"For goodness' sake, spare me. I never heard a girl fly at any one so."

"It's men who act like that, who make girls flirts, and then you blame them."

"We can't help girls being fools."

"You needn't deceive them, and flatter them, and make them think themselves angels."

"They wouldn't if they weren't fools."

"Well, then, if they are not very sensible, you take advantage of them, and that's mean."

"They like it."

"They can't like to be laughed at."

"They don't know it."

"And it's cruel, wicked, to pretend to like them when you despise them."

"How?"

"Suppose they should love you?"

"Flirts never do."

"But before they were flirts?"

"They were born flirts."

"They were not; some one treated them badly, and made them flirts."

"I don't think any one will make a fool of you."

"Perhaps not. I'm out of the way of that sort of people, and now that you've told me I should know *what* it meant."

"Know what *what* means?"

"Compliments."

"They may be sincere."

"I shall always suspect them."

"I tell you that you're looking extremely fresh, and that that great roll, or plait, or whatever you call it, of hair behind your head is very becoming."

"You're my brother."

"Therefore you think I speak truth."

"You wouldn't be likely to compliment me."

"Then truths are not compliments?"

"Not the sort of compliments we were talking of."

"What should you do if people paid you the sort of compliments we were talking of?"

"I don't know; be very angry, I suppose."

"Tell him that he was a fool?"

"No, I don't think; it would be rude, wouldn't it?"

"Yes, but people don't mind that when they're angry."

"I should be very vexed to be made a fool of, shouldn't you?"

"Yes."

"What should you do?"

"If any one trifled with you? Horsewhip him, of course."

Janet clapped her hands. "There, Harry, I've been trying for the last five minutes to make you say that."

"Why?"

"Why, don't you see how unjust you are? You've been calling the poor girls flirts and all sorts of things, to excuse yourself; you would horsewhip anybody who made me think they liked me when they did not, and yet it's what you've been doing yourself by your account."

Harry laughed. "Well, never mind; you haven't asked me about Lucy."

"No, but I want to know."

"You must come and see her."

Janet looked surprised.

"You can come, can't you? I know you have some holiday at Easter. You spent Christmas with the Darrels, surely you can spend Easter with your brother."

Janet said that she would come. She was pleased to see her brother again, and she did not recollect that at the time she most needed help he had stood aloof. Janet had trodden down her worst difficulties; her star was in the ascendant; she would not lack friends now.

"Lucy's name was Leveson; she's my partner's sister."

"Your partner? I did not know that you had one."

"Bless my heart! no, I daresay you didn't; and you didn't know that I had got rid of that office business."

"What! the agency?"

"Yes."

"I thought it was such a good thing."

"That's as people think. It was very well for any one who was satisfied with a moderate income and a humdrum life; office hours from ten to five, and an occasional holiday."

"What are you doing now, then, Harry?"

"Well, the office didn't suit me, and I don't know that I altogether suited the office, though very likely we should have gone on for some time longer if it had not been for a shabby trick Jeremiah Higgins served me; that man can't bear to see any one making money unless he's got a share of the profits, and so——"

"Harry, I think you're unjust; I know Uncle Jeremiah is fond of money, but I don't think he's as bad as that; do you know he sent me ten pounds at Christmas."

"Did he? Well, then, he has a right to ten pounds'-worth of golden opinions from *you*, but he sent *me* no ten pounds."

"I didn't keep his present."

"What did you do with it?"

"Sent it back."

"Whew!! Well, he did me a shabby turn all the same; however, I'm not altogether sorry, as it's turned out. The agency will always be likely to go down. The directors are a set of timid old muffs, who get frightened, and think they're going smash directly they've got an enterprising man of spirit to manage it."

"I don't see that that need follow."

"Of course not, but I'm not telling you what *need* follow, but what *does*."

"You haven't told me what you're doing."

"When some of those banks went wrong I took up bill-discounting; Leveson is my partner. I've been buying a patent also, which I shall turn my attention to, and which I think will be very profitable."

"How was it people sold it? I should have thought they would wish to have kept it if it is likely to be valuable."

"Well, it belonged to a widow; she couldn't work it."

"Did her husband invent it?"

"Yes, if he'd lived he'd have made a fortune."

"What's it to do?"

"Dress flax at about half the usual cost, and to produce a superior quality. Look here. He took from his breast pocket a little book in which were lying little silky skeins of flax."

"I don't understand it, Harry; I dare-say they're very beautiful. Did you make them?"

"No, I haven't got my machinery up, but I *shall* make tons of it."

"I hope you will."

"Now, Janet, about your coming. You needn't say anything about that humbugging school to Lucy."

Harry had made a mistake, and he saw it as soon as he had spoken, but it was too late.

"Harry, if you're ashamed of me I'd rather not come; I can tell no stories." Janet looked about three inches taller than she had done the minute before.

"Stories! no one wants you to tell stories; but you needn't volunteer to Lucy that you're acting as Pratt's school-mistress."

"I'm glad you've spoken about it. I'd

better not come if you're ashamed of me."

"I'm not ashamed of you." She didn't look anything he need be ashamed of.

"I should like to see your home, and Lucy; but you must take the risk of my—my—position being known. Of course I shouldn't go to people and say, I'm Mr Platt's school-mistress and organist, and receive forty pounds a year, it's no business of theirs; but I should make no effort to conceal it."

Harry really wanted his sister to come, therefore he was obliged to put up with the chance of her occupation becoming known. There was one other subject on which he must speak to Janet.

"You'll want some money, and—"

"No, thank you, I have some."

"Hear me out, Janet. Lucy will be giving two or three parties, you'll want some dresses. I shouldn't like you to come in what you have on."

Janet bit her lips. She wished to be friendly with her brother, and to visit him and his wife, yet she felt as if a very little might cause a quarrel; there was nothing very strange in his giving her a dress, but there was more thought for himself than for her in his generosity, and she felt it.

Harry laid two Bank of England notes on the table. "There, Janet, get whatever you require, and mind you look nice. When can you come to us?"

"In ten days. I'll write and tell you the day." She took up the notes. "Thank you, Harry; I'll take care to lay them out to the best possible advantage."

Harry was glad this had been so easily arranged. When she spoke of returning Uncle Jeremiah's present he thought perhaps she might refuse his, and choose to come to Salford in her school dress, or not at all. He looked at his watch; it was nearly time for Janet to return to the school.

"Don't forget to write, Janet. Haven't you any message to send Lucy?"

"Yes; give my love to her."

Harry went to the stable to get his horse, and Janet went towards the village.

CHAPTER VII.

TEN days after Harry's visit to Stoke he might have been seen standing at the door of the principal inn at Salford, waiting for the arrival of one of the coaches. It was a clear, cold afternoon, with a strong east wind blowing. Harry fidgeted, and walked up and down, and looked at his watch, and remarked that the coach was late, and seemed impatient and restless. Janet was coming; he was going to introduce her to his wife. What would she think of her? Harry was accustomed to "gang his ain gate," but he was not indifferent to what Janet would think of his wife. There was a little nervous flutter about Lucy when he had left her, which seemed as though she were not perfectly self-composed. Janet was the first of her husband's family whom she was going to see. It is an awful business being introduced to husband's friends, particularly the female portion of them; it is natural that they should scan and canvass the new relation, and try to discover what sort of a woman the brother or cousin has brought into the family; their habits and prejudices may be very different to what the new-comer has been accustomed to, and they set up a standard by which she cannot be measured, and altogether she stands at a disadvantage.

Mrs Harry Tudor was more favourably circumstanced, inasmuch as she was the hostess, and not the visitor; also Janet was not as formidable as an array of tall grown-up sisters, headed by a mother-in-law.

The coach arrived. Harry directed the porter to bring Janet's boxes, gave his arm to his sister, and they proceeded towards his house.

He had given up the old house with

the office, and had taken a newly-built one at the end of the town.

Lucy heard the house door open; she would like to have run out to meet them, but felt shy. She threw down her worsted work, and went half across the room, and then ran back and reseated herself, and took up her work, but had not set in a stitch before the door opened.

"There, Janet, that's your new sister," was Harry's introduction.

Janet went across the room and kissed her; it was she who must make the first advance to that little fair-haired, blue-eyed creature.

"How long before dinner, Lucy?"

She looked at the time-piece. "An hour, Harry."

"I suppose you two women can take care of each other."

Harry left the room.

"How cold you must be, Janet; do come quite near the fire."

Lucy came towards her.

"Let me take off your gloves; and you'd like to have something before dinner."

"No, thank you; I haven't come far, you know."

"Oh! but do; I shall feel quite uncomfortable; just a glass of wine."

Lucy let go Janet's hand, rang the bell for some glasses, and brought her a glass of wine and a biscuit.

"Untie your bonnet—there—let me put it on the table."

"How kind you are!"

"Kind! oh, no, it's what comes natural to do for any one who has come in cold from a journey. Perhaps you'd like to go to your room now."

"Don't let me take you up-stairs, Lucy, into the cold."

"Yes, please, I should like to go, and it's not cold, because I told Mary to keep up a good fire all day in your room." Lucy took up Janet's bonnet and gloves, and led the way up-stairs.

"Oh, dear! they haven't uncorded your boxes; how very stupid! Perhaps I can do it, though." She knelt down and tried to undo the knots.

"I'll uncord them. You'll hurt your

fingers, Lucy. I'm not used to be so waited on, I assure you."

Janet wished that she hadn't said that. Lucy might think it strange, and she recollected Harry's conversation when he was at Stoke; but Lucy was the most unsuspicious and least inquisitive of people, and took no notice of it.

By their joint efforts the boxes were uncorded. Janet took out a dress, and went to the glass and took down her hair. Lucy fidgeted about the room.

"Can I do anything for you, Janet?"

"Nothing, thank you, but stay, sit down by the fire; I shall not be long dressing."

"Shan't I be in your way?"

"Not in the least."

Lucy sat down by the fire, and watched Janet for some time in silence.

"Janet, before you came I thought I should have been afraid of you, but I'm not."

"Afraid of *me!*" Janet turned suddenly round, and her long, thick hair fell down all over her face. "Afraid of me! Why ever should you be?"

"I daresay you'll think it very silly,

perhaps it was. I thought you were so very clever, and so I believe you are, and I was afraid you mightn't like me because I wasn't like yourself. I shouldn't like Harry's friends to dislike me, you know, or to think me very foolish."

"My dear, kind Lucy, no one would dislike you."

"No, perhaps not quite dislike, but they might think that Harry might have married some one more clever, who could have helped him more."

"I don't quite understand you, Lucy. Harry's business is not such a one as any wife could help him in, and I don't think he wants help if she could."

"I haven't made you understand, that's my fault. I don't know how it is that I should talk to you about all this; an hour ago I had never seen you. I suppose it is because I know that you love Harry, and for his sake would tell me what is right."

"For your own sake too, dear Lucy; but you are quite as likely to know what's right as I am."

"Yes, I know that you're not older than I am, not older in years, but you feel older. You're a woman, and I'm a child."

Janet sighed. There *was* that difference between them.

"I don't think I ever should have married if I'd known how much other people's happiness would have depended on me."

"I'm very glad you did not know it, then."

"No, don't say that; you mean it kind, but don't say it."

"People's happiness depended on you always. Every one in some degree influences the happiness of others."

"Yes, but it's very different being the mistress of a house and being nobody in one's old home."

"I shouldn't think you ever were nobody, Lucy."

"Yes I was, in the way I mean. When poor papa and mamma were alive I had no responsibility; people didn't look to me for orders, and example, and that sort of thing."

"But for Harry's sake, Lucy, you don't mind the responsibility."

"Not the trouble, Janet; don't think I

mind one bit about that, if it were ever so much. It is because I love Harry so much that I am afraid, afraid that I shan't do the best for him. Then he's so clever. I'm afraid I shall never be able to take an interest in things, because I don't understand them."

"What things?"

"Oh! there's a patent he's buying. Did he tell you about it?"

"Yes."

"And I daresay you understood all about it."

"No, I didn't."

"No, really! But you could?"

"I don't know."

"Then you don't think it's because I'm not clever that I don't know all about it?"

"Indeed no; it's Harry's business, not yours. Harry must attend to that, and you must attend to his home, and make it comfortable."

"Ah, that I can do; but there was a lady here a few days ago, and she talked to Harry about it, and went out into the yard to see some of the machinery, and used such learned words. Harry said she was a very clever woman."

"I don't suppose he would like to have her for his wife. I daresay she always has untidy fires, and no buttons on her husband's shirts, only I suppose she has no husband."

"Oh yes, she has, and children too; and one of them was most dreadfully burnt the other day."

"While its mother was examining machinery?"

Lucy laughed. "No, but I believe she was gone to some meeting."

"Well, we must not judge her, but from what you've said I should think a careful study of the last chapter of the book of Proverbs might be useful. King Solomon was a wise man, Lucy."

"Of course, what he wrote is in the Bible."

"Janet was going to have said something, but she stopped. Lucy would not have understood her.

"Janet, to-morrow night we're going to have a party. I used to like parties, but now I get dreadfully nervous lest people shouldn't be amused. You'll help me, won't you?"

"Yes, what can I do?—make custards?"

"No, not that sort of thing; cook does all that; the eating and drinking is the easiest part to arrange; but you know most of the people are strange to me; though my brother is Harry's partner we haven't lived here long. I wish we needn't have parties, but Harry says we must."

"Well, why don't you have a dance? Then they'll amuse themselves, and you need only think of providing a good supper."

"No, that wouldn't do to-morrow night. Harry wishes to know every one. This will be a party of goodies, who would be horrified at dancing."

"Well, will music do? I'll sing to them, or play, anything of that sort."

"Oh! thank you. I'm so nervous I always play worse before anybody."

"Well, after dinner we'll look at your music; perhaps you have some duets."

"I'm so glad you're come. I don't feel nearly as uncomfortable about the party;

but that's a selfish reason. I should have been glad to know Harry's sister always."

Janet kissed her, and the two went hand in hand down-stairs. "You know, Lucy," said Janet, "you must ask the people to play and sing, that will please them more than hearing us."

"I'm sure they're not the sort of people who play well."

"Never mind."

"I can't bear bad music."

"We can bear it for a little while; you can for Harry's sake. It will amuse them, and it won't hurt us."

"But we can't tell them it's good."

"We shan't be asked to do so. If any one played execrably, and asked me if I did not think it beautiful, I should say 'No;' but no one does ask such straightforward questions."

"I wish one need only ask people one liked."

"I don't exactly understand the ground we stand on. I suppose we must sometimes ask uncongenial visitors, just as we perform other unpleasant duties."

"But it feels insincere."

"Not quite that. You may esteem the people, and wish to show them polite attention, although, their minds being altogether different to yours, you would not choose them for daily companions, any more than you would choose a man with one leg shorter than the other as your companion in a long walk."

Lucy threw open the parlour door,—

"Why, Harry, I did not know that you were come back."

"I've been back this half-hour; I suppose you and Janet have been gossiping up-stairs."

"Yes, we've been talking about this awful—"

Harry held up his finger. The servant was bringing in dinner, and he never let Lucy canvass people before servants.

CHAPTER VIII.

THE time-piece in the dining-room chimed a quarter-past six. Mrs Harry Tudor and Janet were seated on either side of the fire, with their feet on the fender.

"Janet, it's of no use putting it off any longer. We must go and dress."

"Yes, I'm going—there." Janet rose and pushed back her chair. "I call that heroism, to leave that lovely fire."

Lucy rose also.

"What must I put on?" asked Janet. "I suppose at home, and especially as you say these are quiet people, we need not array ourselves very gorgeously."

"Why, I don't know, I believe I must put on my wedding-dress. I'd rather wear something else, but I'm afraid they'd think I did not pay them enough respect."

"Will they be very fine themselves?"

"Yes, very fine."

Janet sat down with her elbow resting on the dressing-table when she reached her room; she felt very much disposed to go off into a day-dream instead of dressing, but she roused herself; it was nearly seven, and some of the people might be punctual. There was a knock at the door. It was Lucy.

"Oh! you *are* dressed. Harry wants to see you."

"What about?"

"Only to see how you look."

"Well, I suppose I must indulge him. He gave me this dress, Lucy."

Janet ran down-stairs.

Harry was standing in front of the fire.

Lucy was not pretty, but she was loveable; she looked innocent, and guileless, and good, and there was something delicately nice and lady-like in her white silk dress with its lace trimmings.

"Shall I do, Harry?" asked Janet. "I'm not grand, like Lucy, but then I'm not Mrs Harry Tudor, so it isn't expected of me."

She looked much grander, though she only wore a muslin dress with a Royal Stuart sash.

Harry had no time to make any remark; a carriage drove up to the door.

"There," said Lucy. "There's some one come. Oh dear!"

The drawing-room door opened. Mr and Mrs William Burr, Mr John Burr, Miss Burr, and Miss Prout were announced.

Mr William and Mr John Burr were cousins, who had acquired a comfortable independence in a dry-salting business. Mr William had a screwed-up face; he looked very much like a caricature, and moved his limbs like the limbs of a Dutch doll, at right angles, as if they were fastened together with wooden pins; he jerked out his words, but at the same time was slow of speech, because he had many preambles to get through before he arrived at what he meant to say. Mr John Burr was a large, heavy man with a bald head; Mr

William had frizzled hair. But Mr John had a peculiarity of his own; he grunted between every sentence, or clause of a sentence. Mr William was a married man; his wife was then shaking hands with Mrs Harry Tudor; she was a small mouse-coloured woman, not by any means mouse-coloured in dress, but she had mouse-coloured hair, eyes, and complexion. She would have been kind-hearted if she had not been weak-minded and bigoted. Mr John Burr was a bachelor; he and his sister were both on the wrong side of fifty. She was rather a favourable specimen of a strong-minded woman, for she was kind, and had not the merciless contempt for human weaknesses which is a general attribute of feminine strong-mindedness, if the words are not a contradiction. She was great on school committees and the like; not parish business exactly, because she swore no fealty to Mother Church, but, exercising the right of private judgment, preferred to sit under a certain Mr Swynge, who held forth to an admiring audience in a meeting-house in a side street. Miss Prout was an orphan; she had been brought up by her uncle and aunt; her mother had been their sister; who her father was no one seemed to know, but the report ran that he had been in some way connected with missions, but in what capacity no one definitely said; probably the family knew, but they kept the knowledge to themselves. Miss Prout, on account of these antecedents, was regarded by the congregation of the meeting-house as something half-clerical, and she was invited to meet the deputations from various societies, and the like. She had a hard outline of face, and very black hair, which she wore in three stiff curls on either side of her face. She was made a great deal of by her own family, and by the meeting-house congregation in general, yet it must be confessed that she was an old-young lady, and Miss Prout still, which Mrs William Burr said was surprising. These five people lived near each other, and came to Harry Tudor's house in one fly, Mr John being made to ride on the box. The dress of the ladies would have pleased Aunt Wood; it was substantial, and would probably wear well. They had their own ideas, family ideas possibly, of evening costume, which they resolutely adhered to. They eschewed light fabrics and delicate shades of colour, as also the ordinary shape and appointments of evening dress, preferring to appear in over-trimmed walking dresses. The distinctive mark of full dress seemed, in their idea, to be these trimmings.

Mr William Burr was talking to Harry Tudor, John Burr standing by, grunting at the end of each sentence. Lucy was trying to talk to Mrs William, and Janet sat down by Miss Prout. There was no stiffness about the Tudors, and they were seldom at a loss for the small talk which paves the way to further acquaintance, but with Miss Prout Janet felt herself pulled up and brought to a dead stand; there was scarcely a response to anything she said. Miss Prout sat on the edge of her chair, her hands before her; she looked at Janet, and then at Lucy, and her look said, "I'm sure *you* can't be Christian women either of you." Janet did not wonder that Lucy should dread a party, if it was to be composed of such people as these. She was thankful when she heard announced, "Captain and Mrs Brice." Captain Brice at any rate would be able to say something. Mrs Brice was a little washed-out looking woman, and her husband a tall gentlemanly-looking man; so much Janet saw at a glance, and that there were warm greetings between them and the female Burrs.

"Captain Brice"—no one could say what he was captain of. It is improbable that he had ever handled a gun, still more so that he had ever been on ship-board, except when he crossed with his wife from Dover to Calais, on which occasion he was very ill; but Captain Brice he was called, or rather "the Captain," by his wife's circle of acquaintance. They were great people in their way. Mrs Brice was supposed to possess extreme refinement of taste, and her judgment was appealed to by her acquaintances in delicate cases, where ordinary minds might not be sufficiently discriminating. Mrs Brice was then settling in her mind that Mrs Harry Tudor would be a very sweet young woman, if she could only be brought to sit under Mr Swynge. Janet she considered too *prononcée*. At a later period of the evening she called her pert and flippant. Captain Brice was always at hand to echo his wife's sentiments.

"And how's Miss Rosa, dear Mrs Brice?" said Mrs William Burr.

Janet supposed that the Brices had a daughter.

"You haven't brought her," said Miss Prout.

"No, she wasn't invited." Mrs Brice looked at Mrs Harry Tudor, as though that lady had failed in hospitality.

Janet wondered that Lucy had not invited this pet child.

"Has she been out to-day?" asked Mrs William.

"Not for a walk, the weather has been *too* severe, I feared she might take cold; but she came here with us, and my maid took her back in the carriage."

Miss Prout had playfully seated herself on a low stool at Mrs Brice's feet, and had hold of Mrs Brice's hand as she inquired after Miss Rosa. "And she enjoyed herself the other evening?"

"Yes, she and Miss Fanny at number four got on very well together. I sent Maria with Rosa; I did not like to trust her alone, lest she should eat something which might disagree with her; she's *very* delicate, and a constant anxiety to me, isn't she, Philip?"

Philip drew near to his wife, and said, "A constant anxiety."

"We had a dreadful fright the other day, had we not, Philip?"

Philip said, "A dreadful fright."

"What?" inquired Miss Prout.

"Maria, my new maid, lost her; we didn't know what had become of her for three hours, and *such* hours as they were to me I can't describe."

Philip did not echo as he ought to have done; he was looking at Janet, looking very much as though he admired her.

"I never have let her go out with Maria again since that dreadful day. Philip always takes her her walk after breakfast. I've changed her ribbons, dear; I think rose colour warmer, and more comfortable-looking, this bitterly cold weather, than the blue she had before, don't you?"

"Oh yes! you have *such* taste, dear Mrs Brice," said Miss Prout.

Mrs Brice looked as though she considered it a merited compliment. "Well, I shall always be pleased that such taste as God has given me shall be at the service of my friends."

"Dear Mrs Brice, you are always *so* kind, but about dear Rosa."

"Well, my dear, I'm recovering now; but I haven't had such anxiety since we lost dear Rosa in France; we can never forget that time, can we, Philip?"

This time Philip did echo, "Never."

"You know the particulars, my dear." This was said to Miss Prout. "But this young lady does not." Here Mrs Brice turned to Janet; in spite of her unfavourable opinion Mrs Brice could not resist a new hearer.

"When we arrived at Paris, dear Rosa was not there."

"Why didn't you have her with you?"

"You may well ask; the unfeeling wretches wouldn't let us, separated me from my darling Rosa. We went back to Amiens, she wasn't there, returned to Brussels, and there we found the little darling."

"But, Mrs Brice," said Janet, "why

didn't you *insist* on having her with you? *I* wouldn't have been separated from my child."

"Child!!" exclaimed Mrs Brice.

"Child!!" shrieked Miss Prout.

They looked at Janet as though she had suggested something immoral.

Philip said, dejectedly, "Miss Rosa is a dog."

The room had become full. Mrs Harry Tudor opened the piano, and two young ladies favoured the company by feebly playing a duet set of waltzes, and people said, "Very pretty," "Sweet thing," and Mrs Brice said, "So much feeling," and the young ladies retired, blushing under their laurels. Janet heard beside her, "Do, dear." "No, indeed I couldn't." "My dear, people who have a gift shouldn't be selfish, and keep it to themselves." Then Mrs Brice led Miss Prout to the piano. Miss Prout pulled off her gloves, and tucked them behind the candlestick, looked round imploringly at Mrs Brice, struck two or three chords, coughed, played something like a five-finger exercise, and then sang a little song, in a clear, weak voice, which Mrs Brice applauded much. There was more piano playing, and more singing, and then Lucy came to Janet, and said, "Do you play something, or sing." Janet hesitated a moment what to play; her own idea was that light music was in general best suited to evening parties, but as she had just heard a young lady fall in raptures about Beethoven, she played the march and the concluding fugue from the "Grand Sonata." The people seemed to think that they ought to listen, and to express delight, but they looked extremely bored, all except Mr John Burr, who drew near to the piano, and grunted with satisfaction at every emphatic note, and a pert young man who turned over the leaves, and said, "Very good, very good," in an encouraging, patronizing way.

"Can't you sing something, Janet," said Harry.

A servant came in and went up to Harry Tudor.

"Some one wants to see you, sir."

"Me? Why didn't you say I was engaged?"

"They seemed as if their business was partic'lar."

"Who is it? A gentleman?"

The servant hesitated as to whether or not the stranger was a gentleman.

"Where is he?"

"In the breakfast-room."

"Say I'll be there directly."

This passed while Janet was looking for some music; she turned round to speak to her brother, and he was gone.

She sang, as she always did, with feeling and earnestness, and her rich voice contrasted strangely with Miss Prout's little pipe. The men gathered round the piano, but the women looked at each other affrighted, much as hens would if they descried an eaglet walking about among their chicks.

"Where is Harry? Do you know, Janet? It's supper-time," whispered Lucy.

Before Janet could reply Harry came into the room. His wife and sister both looked at him, and looked away, and looked again. Each thought as she first looked that he was agitated, and as each looked again the thought, what could she have been dreaming of to imagine that that man, who was laughing and joking as he took Mrs William Burr down to supper, could be agitated. Nevertheless Lucy was not quite easy, and as she made her way towards the top of the table she managed to pass near her husband, and to whisper, "Who was it? Who wanted you?" He replied, "No one you know, dear, nothing of any consequence." Lucy was satisfied; if Janet had seen the expression of his face she would not have been satisfied. But Janet did not happen to look at her brother; the table was crowded, and she was trying to make every one comfortable; finally she found a seat reserved for her between Mr John Burr and the pert young man, who had said "Very good, very good," to her playing. She tried to help Lucy in her duties as hostess; what with this, and parrying the compliments, not to say attacks, of the pert young man, who harassed her on one side, and endeavouring not to laugh at Mr John Burr, who grunted much more than usual on the other side, she had no time to think of Harry.

The last guest had departed. Harry, Lucy, and Janet stood by the drawing-room fire.

"Well, it wasn't as bad as I expected," said Lucy, "and you helped me famously, Janet; I'm so much obliged to you."

Harry was looking steadily into the fire.

"Come, Janet, sit down," said Lucy.

"What for? To talk over the people?"

But before Lucy could speak, Harry turned to them,—

"It's time you went to bed, both of you."

"Harry," remonstrated Lucy, "we *must* sit by the fire a little and talk over everything, it's the set-off against a party of heavy people—a duty party, which you said we must have."

"Do you know what time it is?"

"No, never mind about the time. Sit down, Harry, I want you to tell me about some of them; I hardly know who's who."

"As much as you like to-morrow, but not a word will I tell you to-night; come, off with you. There! Janet's yawning, and you're looking pale, Lucy."

"I'm not tired, Harry; we'll stay a little longer."

"Not a minute." Harry lighted a candle for his wife, and one for Janet. "Janet, don't let Lucy stay talking in your room to-night; it's time you were both asleep."

"You horrid tyrant, Harry." Lucy went up-stairs laughing, and Janet followed her.

They reached Janet's room first.

"I do think I'm rather tired," said Lucy. "Good night, dear;" she kissed Janet, and then went on to her own room.

Harry stood by the drawing-room door, in the same spot as when his wife had said, "You horrid tyrant, Harry." He watched her and his sister up-stairs, heard Lucy take leave of Janet, heard Janet's door shut, listened to hear whether Lucy went at once to her own room, or whether any after-thought should make her return to Janet. In a moment he heard

Lucy's door shut, then he seemed greatly relieved; he returned to the drawing-room for a few minutes, as if to collect his thoughts, and then went slowly towards the breakfast-room.

CHAPTER IX.

About the time when Harry Tudor's guests were assembling a shabbily-dressed man stopped at the turnpike, about a quarter of a mile from Salford, and inquired where Mr Harry Tudor lived. It was a bitterly cold night, although in the month of April. The turnpike-man told him to go through the town to the far end of the street, there he would see a new house with big windows, and a brass plate on the door; that was where Mr Tudor lived, and he couldn't mistake it, because the name was on the plate.

The stranger thanked him, and walked on. The principal street of Salford was but badly lighted; a lamp here and there gave just sufficient light to make the general darkness more intense. A carriage with lamps drove past him, rattled past on the hard ground, and pulled up with a dash far at the end of the street; he could just see the bright satin of a lady's dress flash in the lamp-light as she passed from the carriage into the house. On the stranger went. As he approached the end of the street he examined the houses, to find one answering to the description given him,—a new house, with big windows, and a large brass plate on the door. There were none at all like it, until he came quite to the end of the street, to the house before which the carriage had stopped; surely that could not be right, but it was; there was a large brass plate on the door, and by the glare of the lamp in the hall, which shone through the fan-light over the door, he could read the name, H. Tudor. The stranger had his hand on the bell, and then he hesitated, and did not ring, but crossed to the other side of the way, and looked at the house. The shutters in the lower rooms were closed, but he could see that there were lights inside; sharp streams of light came out into the dark street from the cracks of the shutters; above there seemed to be a room with three windows without shutters; the light came glowing into the street through warm-looking crimson curtains. As he stood there the stranger could see that the room was lighted by a chandelier; each light in it looked like a little sun, as it shone against the curtains. The stranger recrossed the street, and again had his hand on the bell, again he hesitated, but at last he rang. No one came, he rang again, a servant opened the door.

"Is Mr Tudor at home?"

The servant said, "Yes." She had been told never to refuse admittance to any one when her master was in the house, but there was hesitation in her manner; she looked at the stranger again and again. Where was she to put him? Supper was being laid in the dining-room; in the breakfast-room were the cloaks and shawls belonging to the guests, she ought not to put him in there, he might steal them; 'twas cold to leave him in the passage;

she was a kind-hearted girl, and her kind heart made her risk the cloaks and shawls; she showed him into the breakfast-room, determining, however, to keep watch, in case "Master" should be long in coming.

The stranger threw himself into a chair by the fire, and watched the door; his mouth twitched and worked uneasily. There were steps in the hall, a hand was on the door, the stranger took his hand from his eyes, but did not attempt to rise. Harry Tudor entered, looking handsome and gentlemanly, with everything well-appointed and nice about his evening dress, and there sat a broken-down man, in a shabby coat, the only one he possessed, and that man was—his father.

Harry held out his hand. Both said something, but what they said was inaudible.

To say that Harry Tudor was glad to have his father come at that time, and in that manner, would be to say what was untrue; and to say that he was not greatly shocked and grieved at his father's appearance would be to do him injustice.

He was greatly embarrassed; not as to

what he should do, but as to *whether* he could carry it out single-handed.

He guessed, and guessed rightly, that his father had done no better for himself abroad than he had done at home, and that he stood in want of everything. It was very inconvenient to Harry Tudor just then to make any additional outlay. Money in abundance was passing through his hands, he wanted it all for his business; his household expenditure was lavish, that was to increase his credit. He was liberal to Lucy; it answered his purpose that his wife should be surrounded with what was pretty and luxurious. Harry Tudor had no great amount of filial affection; he felt that Mr Tudor had greatly failed in his duty towards his family, possibly he thought that in consequence less was required of him; something however must be done; his father must neither want food nor clothing.

The present was an emergency. Here was Mr Tudor arrived most unexpectedly, and making no presentable appearance. Any guest wishing to leave early might come into that room in search of shawl or cloak. He would not like Lucy to see his father as he then appeared, and as to Janet, the thought made him shake, what wild thing might she not do!

Mr Tudor looked exhausted. Harry noticed it. He left the room, met a servant in the hall with a tray of eatables going into the supper-room; he took it from her and told her to bring hot water and glasses into the breakfast-room; he returned, gathered up the shawls and cloaks, and told the servant to take them away.

Mr Tudor watched all that his son did.

Harry placed the tray and the glasses by his father; he fidgeted, he wanted to return to the drawing-room, Lucy would wonder what had become of him, yet he did not wish to wound his father's feelings.

Men circumstanced like Mr Tudor feel differently according to their different temperaments, but they seldom, perhaps never, feel justly. Some become callous, lost to all delicacy, others only the more sensitive, and of this latter sort was Mr Tudor.

"I'm come at an unfortunate time," he said. There was bitterness in the tone.

Janet would have understood it, and

would have answered to the feeling which created the bitterness. Harry understood nothing beyond the actual meaning of the words, and to them alone he replied.

"Well, I've unfortunately got a house full this evening; but it could not be helped."

"Don't let *me* take you from your guests."

Harry looked relieved, still he hesitated to go, then he said,—

"They'll be going before long. No one will disturb you here. I'll come back as soon as they're gone." He pushed the glasses and the tray a little nearer to his father.

Mr Tudor threw himself back in his chair as soon as he was alone. He heard a rich voice singing. He did not recognize it as Janet's, but it was a voice which seemed to speak to all his better feelings; he could picture to himself some bright girl in a home, such a one as he was then in, he looked round the room, warmly carpeted and curtained, with its blazing fire. Why had he not such a home? Why might not Janet be in such a home with him? Time had been when he blamed others, but that time had passed; now, as he bowed his head upon his breast, he said, almost groaned, "Mia culpa — mia massima culpa!"

Then his mood changed, again he looked round the room, and listened to the sounds in the house, but the expression of his face was bitter. Harry could live in luxury, could give expensive entertainments, yet when his father asked him for a little money he always spoke of being pressed. There was money for every one but his father. And here Mr Tudor unnecessarily wounded his own poor bleeding heart; and he did it because he did not understand his son; like the men in the story, Mr Tudor and Harry were looking at different sides of the shield. Mr Tudor regarded that evening's entertainment as so much money spent in pleasure, when Harry said that he had no surplus money; and it was natural enough that he *should* regard it in this manner, because, as far as his own experience went, he knew of no other motive for assembling guests at one's house, and he did not much trouble himself with the affairs of others. Harry Tudor regarded that party solely as a business matter, and the money spent in it just as he would so much money spent in the fittings-up of his office. Not one of the people who were in his house that evening did he ask because he liked them as companions; and it never once occurred to him the light in which his father would regard the proceeding.

Mr Tudor sat still awhile longer. He heard the guests come down-stairs; there was the rustling of dresses, and a murmur of voices, and laughter; he could hear them in the supper-room. The expression of his face became less bitter, but very sad, and two large tears rolled down his cheeks, down his threadbare coat, on to the floor, and he said half aloud, "Oh! Harry, Harry, I've wronged you all, all? But, Harry, if I had such a home as this, and *you* had returned a prodigal, ever so much disgraced, you would have found a home and a welcome. I wouldn't have been ashamed of you;" and he would not. Mr Tudor groaned, and tears again rolled down his cheeks; he thought Harry unkind and unfeeling.

Harry did not mean to be so, although he did not love his father as Janet did. But Mr Tudor's overwrought feelings, over-sensitive because of his position, were deeply wounded. He rose slowly and wearily from his seat; he had tasted nothing, he would taste nothing of Harry's, he would ask nothing further of him; he went to the door, listened, all seemed still outside, he walked quietly through the hall, opened the outer door, and passed out into the dimly-lighted street, unperceived by any one.

Harry, when his guests had departed, and when he believed his wife and sister to be safe in their rooms, went to the breakfast-room, expecting there to see his father, and to his amazement found him gone; everything on the table was untouched. Harry stood still two or three minutes, lost in wonder; the real reason of his father's departure never entered his mind. What should he do? He did not wish to question the servants; he went through all the rooms, went down the street, and in the other way through the yard, and returned almost doubting his senses; doubting whether he had not been dreaming, or at any rate under some species of hallucination. The only thing he could resolve on was to inquire next day of Janet what she knew about her father. She had been with him so short a time that he had had no opportunity of speaking to her alone.

CHAPTER X.

The three bells of Eckington church were doing their best to ring merrily. Dr and Mrs Thorpe had returned home.

Mr Darrel was silent, as he and his mother sat at breakfast on the following morning.

"What are you going to do, Edward? You will be walking down to the rectory presently, I suppose?"

"Yes, shall not you?"

"Yes."

"I think I shall go now, the air feels so warm and sunny."

Stephen was summoned to attend his master. They lingered a little in the garden, and then went through the shrubbery, across the churchyard, and into the rectory garden.

"There's Mrs Thorpe at the window, sir; she sees you, and she's coming out."

Mrs Thorpe came, holding out both hands.

"I'm very glad to see you; and how is your mother, Mr Darrel."

"Very well, she'll call on you presently, at a more reasonable hour. May I come in now?"

"Yes, do. I'm afraid the Doctor can't see you. He's very busy. Stephen, you go round to the kitchen."

"I'm rather glad the Doctor is engaged; I want to see you."

They went in.

"And the change has set the Doctor up?"

"Yes, we've enjoyed it very much. The Doctor is a capital guide. I had never been out of England before."

"I'm glad everything has been so pleasant, but I'm not going to ask you about your adventures now. I wanted to see you alone."

He paused. Mrs Thorpe waited for him to continue.

"Janet Tudor visited us at Christmas."

"Janet Tudor! How ever did you meet with her?"

"We met her at a concert at Derwent. Haven't you heard from her? I know that she has written to you."

"I have not received the letter. We have been moving about, and have missed several letters."

"Janet is not at 'The Vale' with her mother's family."

"Where is she? what is she doing?"

"Living at Stoke, maintaining herself by being Mr Platt's school-mistress and organist."

"Janet! poor child! I wish we had known."

"You could not have prevented it. She is proudly independent."

"Her father is still away?"

"I suppose so."

"And her brothers?"

"Tom is studying medicine. The other is at Salford."

"Doing well?"

"Harry Tudor ought to be, from what we hear of his style of living."

"And you don't think he is; your manner implies as much."

"Not so, Mrs Thorpe; I am in no position to judge of his affairs, but I do think that if he can afford to do as he is doing he ought first to do something for his father and sister."

"And Tom?"

"Talented and popular, from what I hear; but no independence of character."

Mrs Thorpe sighed. "The Doctor will be sorry to hear your opinion of them."

"It was not of them I wished to speak, but of Janet. I want you to go to Stoke and see her, find out all about her. She will tell you more than she would any one else."

"I will go."

"And, Mrs Thorpe, a few hours after she had left, a gentleman called to see her; he came here first, thinking she was visiting you."

"A young man, of course, and I'm to find out all about him. Oh, Mr Darrel!

Mr Darrel! don't talk about women being inquisitive!"

But when Mrs Thorpe looked up, there was such a shadow on his face that she ceased all jesting.

"You shall have my pony-carriage, and Stephen to drive you."

"Thank you, but can't the Doctor drive me?"

"No, you'll do better without him."

"Well, why shouldn't *you* go? I'll drive *you*."

"No, you'll do best alone. Stephen shall drive you, and you'll go soon."

"Yes."

And he went away.

CHAPTER XI.

Two or three days after Mr Darrel's visit to Mrs Thorpe, Stephen might have been seen driving that lady in the little pony-carriage along the road towards Stoke.

Mrs Thorpe was sorely perplexed as to whether Janet had acted well or ill.

Dr Thorpe said, "Suppose you set the matter aside, and suspend judgment until you have seen Janet."

But Mrs Thorpe did not find it possible to set a matter aside in which she had a deep interest.

"Mr Darrel seemed to think Janet right," said Mrs Thorpe.

"I should depend more on what his mother said," replied her husband.

"Mrs Darrel spoke highly of her, but there was something queer about her manner. Didn't you notice it?"

Dr Thorpe did not say whether he noticed it or not, but he recommended his wife to go and see her old pupil as soon as possible.

When Mrs Thorpe reached the farm Grace was as usual bustling and busy; she stayed a moment to finish what she was doing, and then went to the door to see who could have knocked.

"Bless me! if it isn't Miss Browne, Mrs Thorpe I mean, begging you pardon, an' hoping no offence, which is very likely I might make a mistake, as I haven't seed you since you was Miss Browne. Do 'ee come in, ma'am, an' I hopes the Doctor 's well."

Mrs Thorpe went in.

"An' only to think o' your catching me in this mess; an' Mrs Harris is gone to Derwent, an' I wer' jist a-going to clean myself.'

"Never mind, Grace, you always *are* clean."

"You came to see Miss Janet?"

"Yes. We only returned last week."

"Ah! I he'rd as how you'd been in forin parts. I knowed else you'd ha' come an' seed Miss Janet, an' then p'raps things wouldn't ha' been as they is."

"Is Janet here now?"

"Not in th' house, she's at the school." Grace looked at the clock. "She'll be home in half an hour, unless she goes into the church to play the orgin. I'll send the boy an' tell her to make haste."

"No, Grace. Don't hurry her, I shall be glad to talk to you about her, if you can spare the time."

"Spare the time! I should think I could. Who should I spare time for, if it weren't for Miss Janet. Mrs Thorpe, 'tisn't *my* fault that Miss Janet's a-demeaning herself like this. 'Tisn't *my* fault. I'd ha' kep' her like a lady, if she'd ha' let me. Nor John Harris didn't want for her to pay him nuffin. She wer' welcome to what she had. He's well-to-do, an' he's got no children. But she *would* work, an' *wouldn't* be indebted to nobody. Some gets prouder the poorer they is, an' Miss Janet's one on'em. Only don't blame *me*, Mrs Thorpe. I'd ha' kep' her like a lady, if she'd ha' let me."

"No one blames you, Grace."

"Well, I hope they mayn't; but how did you hear, ma'am, as Miss Janet were here?"

"Mr Darrel told me. Now I want to hear about her; he told me what he knew, but that wasn't much."

"Well, Mrs Thorpe, you knows how master went an' left her. I can't bear to tell on it; he wer' always a kind master to me, an' kind to Miss Janet, an' fond o' her too. When I mind the day afore he went away, I do think it a'most broke his heart to leave her. Ther', 'twer' no good sorrowing then, he should ha' thought what 'twould come to long afore. Them Higginses mad' him worse, not but that missis were a nice lady, you mind her, Mrs Thorpe? but Mr Jeremiah an' Mrs Wood is dreadful, an' master had been brought up different to they, so 'twer' always uncomfor'able. 'Tweren't out of any love to she that they took Miss Janet to 'The Vale,' but because they wouldn't like for it to be said that any o' their kin wanted, or had to work for their livin'. I know 'twer' that, by the way Mr Jeremiah an' Miss Delia spoke to her."

"What made her come away?"

"Why, they mad' her feel as how she wasn't wanted. An' they was always a-telling her how her father owed 'em money; an' they mad' her feel as all they did was done out o' charity."

"Then they didn't like her coming here?"

"I should think they didn't. Mr Jeremiah comed over here, an' wanted her to go back wi' him; he said as how things should be all pleasant, if only she'd come back; you see he were afraid what people might say."

"And she wouldn't?"

"No; she spoke very civil, an' said she were very much obliged for what they'd done for her, but she'd mad' up her mind she'd better stop, an' she wer' right. Mr Jeremiah could no more stop Mrs Wood's tongue than he could dam up yon mill-stream wi' a cabbage-stalk."

"Well, Grace?"

"He went away, then, an' I 'spec' he

spoke his mind to Mrs Wood when he got home, for he wer' very angry, I know that by the way he twitched his reins from off of the gate; I wer' looking out o' winder. 'Twer' Mrs Wood that behaved so very unkind to Miss Janet. I don't suppose she'd ha' come away if it hadn't a-been for her."

"Where are her brothers?"

"I believe Mr Tom's in Edinburgh, or Lonnon, or some place, larning to be a doctor; he might be a doctor by this time for aught I know. She hears from him sometimes, but not often, an' I don't know much about him. Mr Harry's grown a fine young man. I used to be very proud o' them boys, but somehow I don't believe there's either one so good as Miss Janet."

"Doesn't Mr Harry come to see his sister?"

"He didn't for a long time; he wer' angry wi' her for what she were doing, an' he didn't think John Harris's house grand enough for her. No more it isn't; but before he found fault he should ha' found her a better. 'Tis very easy for him to say, 'You must knock under, an' not be so proud, an' you must live at The Vale;' he doesn't know what 'tis he's telling her to do, she's bore more nor ever he would; an' a'ter all, when he says, 'You should do this, an' you shouldn't do the other,' 'tisn't for her good nor comfort that he speaks, but because it hurts his pride that his sister should do this an' that. Howsomever, I 'spose he's thought better on it, for he comed to see her a'ter he were married, an' she went to stop wi' him at Easter, an' I believe she likes her new sister very much."

"He's getting on very well, isn't he?"

"So some do say, an' others not. He rides a fine horse. People say him an' his uncle ha' quarrelled, an' all sorts' o things they do say."

"Then he did not wish his sister to live with him, though he found fault with her being here. How was that?"

"I don't know nuffin about it, Mrs Thorpe; excep' if he's so rich as one would think, there's many things as he ought to do which he don't do; an' if he isn't rich he's a foolish young man to do as he does, an' I don't believe as any good 'll come of it."

"Who was that who came to see Miss Janet a few weeks ago? He came to our house at Eckington, thinking that she was visiting us."

"Did he? That were Mr Bateman's son, Mr Andrew, an' that's another thing I trouble about. Mr Tudor an' Mr Bateman were great friends when we lived at Holme. I always thought that Mr Andrew had took a liking to Miss Janet, an' I believe he had, an' I believe she liked him. Then, you see, when master's troubles comed everything were different, an' I believe Mr Andrew's father won't let him have Miss Janet."

"Miss Janet is late, isn't she?" said Mrs Thorpe, looking at the clock.

"Yes, you'd better let me send for her. Oh! there she is, a-coming in at the yard gate."

"There's some one as wants to see you, Miss Janet; some one as you didn't espec'," said Grace from the door.

Grace went up-stairs to tidy herself.

Janet came into the kitchen.

"Mrs Thorpe! when did you return?"

"Only last week."

"Did you get my letter?"

"No."

"How did you know that I was here?"

"Mr Darrel told me. He asked me to come and see you."

Janet coloured very red, which did not escape Mrs Thorpe's notice, and she remembered Mrs Darrel's curious manner.

Janet thought, Surely she isn't come on a mission from Mr Darrel.

After her conversation with Grace Mrs Thorpe had thought that all mysteries were unravelled; now the threads were again becoming entangled.

"Have you been here long?"

"Yes, and have heard a great deal about you from Grace. I must go soon, I have a long ride home, but I shall come and see you again before long."

"No, Mrs Thorpe, stay a little."

Janet sat down in her old place on the settle.

"Mrs Thorpe, you don't blame me very much for what I've done?"

"As far as actions go, I don't blame you at all, Janet. You yourself best know what your motives have been, and how far you have let pride influence you. I wish I could find you an easier life."

"I do very well, Mrs Thorpe; I shouldn't be any happier in an easier life, as you call it."

"What *do* you mean?"

"Why, you know that I have many things to trouble me. If I hadn't so much to do I should brood over them more."

Strange girl, thought Mrs Thorpe.

"Your visit to Eckington was a nice change. Did you enjoy it?"

"Yes, very much."

"Should you like to go there again? But it will be our turn to have you next."

"Thank you; but I shall not be able to leave Stoke for some time."

Janet spoke constrainedly. Mrs Thorpe felt sure that something more than common had happened while she had been at Eckington. Janet was trying to think of something to say, but she could think of nothing. She felt certain that the subject she desired to avoid would be touched on.

Mrs Thorpe said that she must go, yet she lingered on.

"Janet," she said, "what is it that

causes this constraint in your manner, and in Mrs Darrel's also? Tell it me; whatever it may be, you know that I wouldn't ask from curiosity."

"If *they* haven't kept their secret I suppose I needn't, but I did not wish to tell any one."

"They have told me nothing."

"Somehow you have found it out. Oh! Mrs Thorpe, it hasn't been my fault, indeed it hasn't. I'm *so* sorry for him."

Janet hid her face and cried bitterly; and before Mrs Thorpe went away she knew all about Janet's two love stories.

CHAPTER XII.

THE home-life of Andrew Bateman and his father had been changed ever since the day when the latter had forbidden Janet's name to be mentioned. To the casual observer no difference might have been apparent. Mr Bateman was liberal, and in many ways considerate, towards his son, and Andrew was attentive to his father; people might have thought how happy the two were in each other. But Andrew had ceased to seek or to find happiness in his home; he did not respect his father's opinion and judgment as he used to do. Was he not prejudiced? Did he not steadily refuse to open his eyes to conviction? So

Andrew never attempted to argue with his father on any subject; he heard all that he had to say in a perfectly respectful manner, and if he differed in opinion the subject dropped; his silence meant,—it's of no use arguing with a man who does not sift out the truth, but who grounds his arguments on preconceived notions, which are as likely to be wrong as right.

Mr Bateman felt the change, but was perfectly satisfied with what he had done. So far from altering his opinion, he was more than ever confirmed in the belief that he was right; for, from what he heard, he did not believe that the young Tudors, Janet's brothers, would do any good for themselves.

Andrew and his father were in the counting-house.

Some one said, "Where can I find Mr Bateman? Is he disengaged?"

The voice and manner of speaking were both very different to those of the people who usually came there.

Mr Bateman and his son both looked up and listened. The voice was familiar, yet they could not recollect whose it was.

The clerk who had been addressed said, without raising his eyes from his ledger, "You'll find Mr Bateman in at the first door to the right."

The stranger followed the direction.

"Doctor Thorpe!" exclaimed both Mr Bateman and his son.

Whatever differences might exist, they were unanimous in giving the Doctor a hearty welcome.

"And what brings you to Holme, Doctor?"

"Business."

"And you are better for your holiday?"

"Yes, quite well, thank you. We have scarcely been at home a fortnight."

"And Mrs Thorpe?"

"Quite well; she has enjoyed her trip wonderfully; but I must not keep you talking now, you are engaged."

"How long do you stay?"

"Until to-morrow."

"Is there anything we can do for you?"

"Yes, I think there will be presently."

"Well, Doctor, whenever we can be of service you'll let us know, and you'll dine with us."

"Thank you." The Doctor turned to Andrew, "Can you come with me for an hour?"

"Yes, for as many as you please." He took up his hat, and they went out together.

They could not talk in the crowded streets.

Andrew went whither the Doctor led. They soon left Holme, and reached the borders of the common.

"Where are you going?" said Andrew. "There are no houses further on."

"Suppose my business should be with you! We can talk it over while we walk across the common and home by the river; it used to be a favourite walk of mine when you were my pupil at the old Grammar School."

They walked on a short time in silence. Andrew guessed what was the subject of the business, but did not like to say a word; and the Doctor felt a difficulty in beginning.

"I'm sorry we were not at home when you came to Eckington, Andrew. Whom did you call to see?"

"Janet Tudor. You know all, I'm sure you do."

"Perhaps I may know something, but I wish to hear more from yourself. I have a great friendship for you, boy, and Mrs Thorpe and myself feel something more than friendship for that dear child, fatherless as well as motherless we may consider her, and if harm came to her, which we could prevent, we should never forgive ourselves."

"Harm, Doctor! You don't suppose I'd harm her! I'm as jealous for Janet Tudor's good name as ever *you* can be! If it wasn't for the miserable prejudice of some one who ought to know better, I should have a better right than any one to protect her."

Andrew's cheek flushed, and he spoke angrily.

"Hush! No one has ever called in question Janet's good name, but there are many ways of harming her. If there is no possibility of this affair ever coming to the termination you hope, better let it be given up; don't see her to unsettle her; don't give rise to delusive hopes in her mind."

"Did Janet send you to say this?"

"No; she does not know of my coming."

"Doctor, you think me selfish, you

think that she would make greater sacrifices than I. It may be true. She's an angel, if ever there was one, but you don't know what you ask."

"She's no angel, but a very nice girl, and a spirited girl, but I ask nothing of you; I came here to serve you both, to see whether what I may be able to say will not remove your father's prejudices."

Andrew shook his head, and there was a long pause.

"You can't reason with my father," Andrew said after a while, "he's wholly unreasonable. Because Mr Tudor did as he did he pronounces all the family to be bad, sets down Janet as a designing, mercenary girl, and forbids her name to be mentioned. What can you do after that? It's my belief that he was as unreasonable in his friendship for Mr Tudor as he now is in his prejudice against the whole family. I was a boy at the time, and then I went away from home, but I daresay if I could have seen all, and had been capable of judging, I should not have found all the good in Mr Tudor which my father chose to imagine."

"There may be some truth in what you say, but you must not judge your father harshly. If I am able to form a more correct judgment, it is partly because I have not so much at stake as he has, and partly because I am better acquainted with Janet Tudor than he is."

"He has known her as long as you have."

"Perhaps; nevertheless, he may not have had as many opportunities of observing her as I have."

"It would have been all the same."

"That you can't tell. Supposing your father not to possess great insight into character, that is his misfortune rather than his fault. It would be happier for him to sanction your wishes than to have things going on as they now are."

"I don't know. He's made up his mind that he won't. You can't convince an obstinate man, because he won't be convinced."

"Andrew, you must not let anything estrange you from your father."

"Doctor, why should he come between me and—my wife."

"Poor boy! poor boy! I'm sorry for you, sorry for you all," and he laid his hand on Andrew's arm. "But you must not let a disappointment make you unjust. After all, is it not his love for you which causes what you think his prejudice?"

"No, Doctor, not all. It's an unbending will, which won't be convinced."

"But which I shall try to convince before the day is over."

Each followed his own thoughts for some time in silence. They had reached the path by the river where Andrew had first told Janet of his love.

Andrew suddenly stopped. "Doctor, if you were to get my father to give his consent, there is still another obstacle."

"What do you mean? You have no rival?"

"No, I do not doubt her love, but there may be a feeling even stronger."

The Doctor looked inquiringly.

"Yes, there may be, her pride, pride which says, 'I won't bring disgrace into any family.'"

"Disgrace! Janet! I don't understand."

"More credit for you that you don't. Janet was made to feel, day by day, hour by hour, in that cursed life which she led at 'The Vale,' that her father's short-comings are a disgrace which clings to *her*. *My* father's treatment of her has increased the feeling, no doubt. Her own sense must tell her that she is not responsible for the faults of another, but she has been taught to believe that the world thinks otherwise, therefore she is very likely to say, 'No one shall have it in their power to say that *I* brought disgrace on them.'"

"But, Andrew, if she loves you as you think, she will make pride knock under."

"Once she would, but the last two years have increased her pride."

"And her love too."

"But the pride; I'm not sure that her very love won't strengthen her pride. She is very likely to say, 'There can be no love in bringing disgrace on the person I most love.'"

"Is that what she told you at Stoke?"

"Something like it."

They had reached the outskirts of the town.

"Well, Andrew, I shall see you again this evening; six o'clock, isn't it? your dinner hour I mean."

Andrew went through the streets back to the counting-house. The Doctor retraced his steps a little way, and sat down on a sheltered spot by the river-side. He had come to Holme hoping to be able to serve three people for whom he felt a sincere friendship. He had thought that he understood all the bearings of the case; but here was an aspect of affairs for which he was quite unprepared. He had come expecting to find Mr Bateman hard to convince; but he did not dream of Janet raising an objection. He had had but little experience in woman-kind; the course of his own love had run smooth, and his courtship had been uneventful. If with private individuals, as with nations, those whose history is the least exciting is the happiest, the Doctor and his little wife must have appropriated an undue share.

He sat there mechanically pulling the long grass, and watching it float down the stream. He wished Mrs Thorpe had been with him; he almost thought that she might be able to manage matters better than he could, at any rate he would have been glad of her opinion. Suppose, after all, that Janet *should* hold out! Then he tried to think why people with happiness within their grasp should cast it aside. Did not every one do so more or less? He tried logically to prove, that since Janet loved Andrew, she would not let any other feeling prevent her marrying him, supposing Mr Bateman could be induced to give his consent, and after a most perfect chain of reasoning he was obliged to confess that logic and the feelings of woman-kind had no affinity, and that Janet Tudor might after all let pride gain the day. "Oh!" groaned the Doctor, "I could manage a hundred boys, but I can't manage one woman." He rose from the grass and walked towards the town. "Women are *not* reasonable," he said to himself; then he felt self-condemned, he had been *so* happy, it was like finding fault with his happiness to malign women, even in thought. "No matter for that, they are *not* reasonable, very unreasonable, and unreasoning too, even Mrs Thorpe is that, and she's the best woman in the world."

CHAPTER XIII.

Dr Thorpe and Mr Bateman sat a long time in the old dining-room.

"Fill your glass, Doctor, it's like old times; I wish we had you among us again."

"My post is well filled."

"I have nothing to say against your successor, but old people don't like changes."

Andrew rose.

"Going out this evening, Andrew?"

"Don't you remember that meeting; you said yesterday that one of us had better go."

"Never mind, we don't see the Doctor every day, sit down."

"I think I'll go, father; I shall see you again presently, Doctor;" and he went out.

"Good boy that, never neglects a duty. If education has done it, we owe you a great deal."

"Education does something, no doubt, and home training more."

Mr Bateman sighed.

The Doctor had forgotten to fill his glass. The same subject under different aspects occupied both minds.

Dr Thorpe knew that Andrew would not so rigidly have attended to business that evening had he not known that he wished to see his father alone. It was a difficult subject to begin, one requiring tact. If he did not do good, he would most likely do harm.

Mr Bateman's own remark seemed a little to open the way, therefore the Doctor continued Andrew's praise.

"Andrew *has* been a good son; he has never intentionally given you cause for uneasiness?"

"Never, Doctor; he's stiff in his opinions sometimes."

"Most people with any character are."

"Ay, he's a good lad, take him altogether; I've no cause to find fault with him. You've not filled your glass."

Dr Thorpe filled his glass; very slowly he did it, thinking all the time whether he had not better tell Mr Bateman plainly the reason of his visit to Holme.

Mr Bateman himself continued,—"And yet I *am* anxious about him. It will be lonely for him when I am gone. I should like to see him married, to know that he has a good wife."

"A very natural wish. Won't he marry?"

Mr Bateman did not reply for a minute; when he did his face was flushed and his voice agitated.

"I'm afraid he won't. He was entangled once by that rascal Tudor's daughter. She has come between me and my son ever since."

"How?"

"How! Can you ask how? Why, Andrew falls in love with her; he's clever enough, but he's no match for a designing woman. He swears she's a piece of perfection. I call her an artful minx. She's got a very pretty face, I must own that. He wants to bring her home as Mrs Andrew. I'm an old man, and not so easily imposed on. *I* see through the girl. I was taken in once by her father, and 'a burnt child fears the fire.' Andrew, of course, thinks me unjust and cruel; it would be more cruel to let my son ruin himself, be beggared by a lot of unprincipled pauper relations."

"And what says the young lady?"

"Why, the young lady has a keener eye to business than ever her father had. She is perfectly aware that, if she married Andrew without my consent, she would marry a poor man, so she very prudently declines. Andrew told me this himself, poor lad, as a mark of her disinterestedness and sense of filial duty, so you may fancy how far gone he is."

"Where is Miss Tudor now?"

"Goodness knows, flirting with some one else, most likely."

"Bateman, you and I are old friends; will you listen to me? I told you that I had come to Holme on business; that business was none of my own, but was about your son and my dear young friend, Janet Tudor."

"They're not married, Doctor?"

"No, nor likely to be, without your knowledge and consent. Therefore, don't alarm yourself."

"If you think to alter my opinion, I can spare you the trouble. I have all faith in your integrity, but you are deceived; I won't see my son ruined."

"I should be very sorry to ask you to see your son ruined. You think Janet Tudor mercenary and scheming, and—"

"I *know* it."

"What if I could tell you that she had refused a man whose position and wealth were greatly superior to your son's?"

"You can't; I don't believe it!"

"You would believe it if you heard it from the man himself."

"Some rascally old *roué*, probably; whom to marry would be to lose cast, and she knows it."

"No, a man about your son's age, of unsullied character."

"Touched in the head, imbecile."

"A man with a fine mind, highly cultivated."

"Perhaps, like my son, he would have married her poor, because without his friends' consent. There must have been some reason for her refusing him."

"Of course there was; but his property was entailed, therefore he loses nothing by pleasing himself; but in this instance his mother wished it."

"They don't know the disgrace which is attached to the name."

"If you mean her father's affairs, they know all; but they are sufficiently just not to blame the daughter for the father's faults."

Mr Bateman winced, but he said, "Well, I am glad that she has such chances; it will be something for her to boast of. They can afford to be generous; they have not been wronged as I have been. You haven't told me why she refused, though I don't know that Miss Tudor's affairs are any business of mine."

"You say, truly, they have not been wronged as you have been wronged, but cannot you be generous? Janet Tudor has had no hand in your wrong. Bateman, you are wronging an innocent girl; she is not the one to boast of these things. If something had not led us to suspect it, Janet would never have told us of it. She refused a marriage which many girls would have caught at, simply because she loves your son; but she is as proud as you can be; she would never enter a family to be looked down on."

"And you believe all this?"

"As I happen to be intimately acquainted with all parties, I cannot be mistaken."

"Her father and brothers are no great things."

"That makes her neither better nor worse."

"When did you see her?"

"I have not seen her since our return; my wife saw her last week. I wish we could persuade her to live with us."

"Why doesn't she?"

"Because she is very independent, and won't be indebted to any one while she can work for herself. Besides her daily occupation, she is trying to educate herself more highly, that she may be able to get a better salary, and be able to save money towards paying her father's debts."

"By God! if what you say is true she's a plucky girl. It's a bad family all the same. Where is she?"

"At Stoke."

"Doing what?"

"Acting as Mr Platt's village-schoolmistress and organist."

"Living by herself?"

"No, that old servant, Grace, lives there; Janet is with her."

"How came she to leave 'The Vale?' I thought her mother's family took to her."

"They made her so uncomfortable that she could not stay. She went to Grace, and took the first situation which offered, and has been working on ever since."

"Supposing your opinion of her to be correct—mind, I don't say that it is correct, I only say, *supposing* it to be,—it's not a very pleasant family to be connected with."

"You can't have everything as you would wish it."

"You would not like it for a son of your own, Doctor?"

"If I had a son I should be well pleased that he should marry Janet Tudor. Can you not overlook the father's fault, if a man in a position superior to your own can do so."

"I may be more sensitive than he. We men of business are some of us *very* sensitive."

"No one can be more sensitive than the man I am speaking of, where right and honour are touched."

"Perhaps his position is such that he can afford to do as he pleases better than I."

"Bateman, you're not one to bow to the world's opinion in matters of importance; at least, you used not to be."

Andrew came in. The Doctor found that it was getting late, and rose to go. Mr Bateman would like to have said, "Thank you, old friend; right or wrong, I know that your motive in coming has been good and true." But Andrew was there, so he shook the Doctor's hand in silence.

Dr Thorpe stepped out into the warm air of the summer night, fearing that his visit had not effected much. He would return home on the morrow, and take counsel of his little wife.

CHAPTER XIV.

At the close of a stormy autumn day, Janet sat in her old place trimming a bonnet. It was a market day. The farmer and his wife had returned wet and weary from the neighbouring town. John Harris sat a shorter time than usual with his pipe, and Mrs Harris's knitting was not produced.

The farmer and his wife had disappeared. Grace sat on the opposite side of the fire to Janet.

"Miss Janet, you aren't going to sit up late? Leave that till to-morrow."

"I shan't be late, but I should like to finish it to-night."

Grace looked tired.

"Don't sit up for me, Grace; you're always tired on market days."

Grace protested against such being the case. She sat dozing by the fire for some time, at last she got up, protested that Miss Janet would kill herself working like that, and then went to bed.

Janet's fingers moved busily, her thoughts were busy likewise. The house was very quiet. The only audible sounds were the ticking of the clock, the chirp of the crickets, and the sigh of the wind outside.

She had not heard from her father for a long, long time; she doubted whether her last letters had reached him, and hesitated to write again to the same address. She had suffered more acute pain when first the knowledge of her father's position came upon her, but now a dull leaden pain seemed gathering round her, hard to bear, hard to bear from the hopelessness of the case.

She had said to Mrs Thorpe, that if she had less to do she would brood over her troubles more, and she said truly. Hitherto she had been marking out a path for herself since she had left "The Vale." The details were not precisely those she would have chosen, but the independence of the life suited her well. There had been a certain amount of excitement about it likewise, and the whole course of her every-day experience had been gilded by the thought of her father and Andrew; by her care for the one, by her love for the other. She had heard nothing of Andrew for a long time. Why should she? She knew not where her father was. The post of village-schoolmistress looked very different to her now to what it had done a year before; even the notes of the organ sounded less sweet to her, and the music of the great masters less inspired. And now began true heroism, the working on, accepting as a duty the labour which each day brought, without the excitement of love, without the cheering hope which had hitherto prevented the full weight of the burden from being felt.

She sat there alone, working and thinking of all that had happened, and of her present life; and How long can this state of things last? was the question which arose in her mind. She did not expect any pleasant change; at that moment such did not seem possible, certainly very improbable. It cannot last long, she thought to herself, and in saying this she did not mean the great change, she did not mean to assert in a despairing way, "A hundred years hence it will be over; this state of things, with myself, will have passed away, and will be forgotten," neither did she mean to say that this state of things would kill her, that she should die soon; she thought nothing of the kind, but merely she intuitively perceived, rather than at that moment reasoned from past experience, that nothing *does* last long in precisely the same order, a change *does* come, whether we will it or not, and that when least we expect it.

The bonnet was finished, all but pinning in the cap. Janet set it on the table, shaded her eyes from the light, and sat for some time doing nothing but thinking. Then she took a letter from her pocket; it was from Tom. She read the letter, again she shaded her eyes from the light and sat thinking; there was an impatient drawing up of the breath, and impatience also in the way she tapped her foot against the floor. She did not like Tom's letter at all; there was a parade of work, a hint of dying in harness. If he had suddenly appeared before her she would have snubbed him, she would have said, "Nonsense, a young, strong man to talk like that, pitying himself, indeed!" And then her face softened, and a tear stood in her eye; she was thinking of the old days, and Tom was very dear to her, dearer than ever Harry had been. She made up her mind to write encouragingly to Tom, even though she told him that he must work. After all, the snubbing process would have been more what he deserved. If he wrote dismally, it was not that he was overworked, nor that he was without good chances of success, but because he neglected duties, and was dissatisfied with himself, as those must be who feel their lives to be a sham and a mockery.

And Harry—"Poor Harry," she said, and smiled at herself for saying *poor* Harry—was he not getting on wonderfully? Somehow it felt as though it could not all be real. She must be becoming nervous and fanciful. She returned to her own practical life, put up her work things, and took up a book which Mr Platt had lent her. As she sat alone, in that very still room, she heard a sound, it seemed like some one trying to find the door. She listened, all was still, it must have been a branch of the rose-bush blown against the window; again she heard it; she rose from her seat in the settle, and stood in the middle of the kitchen listening; there *was* some one. She opened the door; the wind almost extinguished her light; she sheltered it with her hand, and before her, in the darkness, could just distinguish a dripping figure, but whether it was man or woman she could not tell.

CHAPTER XV.

The dark object which Janet saw before her when she opened the door was a man. When the light shone on him she recognized him as a labourer from a neighbouring farm. He fumbled among his wet clothes, and at last drew from his pocket a letter, which he gave Janet, wished her "Good night," and vanished in the darkness. There was a pond in the yard; she stood a minute holding open the door, listening for the click of the gate, which would assure her that the man was safe, and had not in the darkness wandered into the pond; then she returned to the kitchen and opened the letter. She did not at first recognize the writing.

It was from Lucy; very incoherent, evidently written under excitement; all she could understand was that Lucy entreated her to come to her without delay; but she gave no hint of what her distress was, and Janet took it for granted that it *was* distress which made her write thus. It was close upon midnight, every one in the house but herself was in bed; it was blowing a tempest outside, she could do nothing until morning; surely Lucy would not expect her that night. She looked at the letter again, but could understand nothing more than she had done on the first reading. She must go to Salford. She did not at all like asking Mr Platt for a holiday, but there was no avoiding it, and at last she went to bed, and to disturbed, unrefreshing sleep.

Janet came down-stairs on the following morning with a little carpet-bag in her hand. Grace was in the kitchen alone.

"Grace, I had a letter after you were gone to bed last night. I must go to Salford to-day."

Grace looked surprised.

"I think I ought to have had the letter earlier."

"'Twas that good-for-nothing Joe Smith brought it, I'll warrant; he did go to market yesterday. I'll talk to him when I see him; biding about, spending his money, an' keeping folk's letters!" This Grace said to relieve her own mind; she was surprised at this sudden move, and saw that it would be useless to question Janet about it.

"How shall you go, Miss Janet,—by the coach?"

"Yes, and I must see Mr Platt as soon as I've had my breakfast."

Janet's breakfast was soon finished, and she walked quickly along, as though she had an unpleasant duty to perform, which she determined to get over as quickly as possible.

Mr Platt was not dressed when she arrived at the Vicarage. It was some time before he made his appearance.

"Good morning, Miss Tudor; I'm sorry to have kept you waiting. You're an early visitor."

"Yes. Will you give the children a holiday? I'm sorry to ask it, but I *must* go to Salford. I can't help it; I will be back to-morrow."

She spoke hurriedly and abruptly, as if it was a great effort, and put Lucy's letter into his hand.

He read the letter.

"I'm very sorry to ask for a holiday. I don't at all know what she means, but I think I must go after receiving this."

"Certainly, Miss Tudor. The children won't object to a holiday, and if you find it desirable to remain, don't feel obliged to return to-morrow."

"Thank you, Mr Platt, I'm *very* much obliged to you."

Mr Platt could not help smiling, she said "very much obliged" in such a proud way, as though the obligation was very disagreeable to her.

"You'd better come and see Mrs Platt, and have some breakfast."

"Thank you, I breakfasted an hour ago."

She wished him "good morning," left the house, and went towards the sign-post which the coach passed. She had not long to wait; she got in, and in two hours reached Salford. No one met her; she was not surprised at that; Lucy probably had expected her the evening before. Janet walked to her brother's house. Everything looked as usual, only there was an air of mystery about the servant who opened the door, when she said her master was from home, that her mistress was up-stairs; she would tell her that Miss Tudor was come; would she please to walk into the dining-room.

The dining-room table was strewed with papers and writing materials. The position of the chairs suggested the idea that five or six people had lately occupied them. A young man was seated with his back to the table, his feet stretched towards the fire, and his hands in his trowsers pockets; his face wore a troubled expression; he looked as if he had just turned from the heap of papers behind him.

Janet guessed that this must be Lucy's brother; there was a likeness to his sister, but he had been from home at the time of her previous visit, so that she had never seen him.

He rose, took his hands out of his pockets, and bowed, when Janet entered.

"Mr Leveson, I suppose."

He bowed again.

Janet gave him Lucy's letter.

He read it, and uttered an exclamation of impatience. "I told her not to send for you, it could do no good. When did you receive this?"

"Late last night."

"By whom?"

"By a man who lives at Stoke. I can't think how he came by it."

Janet glanced round the room, at the papers, at Mr Leveson.

"Is Lucy ill?"

"No."

"Where is Harry?"

"From home."

"Mr Leveson, what is the matter? what does it all mean? Something is the matter. Why did Lucy send for me? Shall I go to her?"

Janet was moving towards the door, as though she would go to Lucy.

"I desired Lucy not to write, but it seems that she has done it. These things are not a woman's business."

"Mr Leveson, if you have any mercy,

tell we what is the matter at once; most likely I must know it sooner or later."

He hesitated still.

"If you are afraid of a scene, you needn't be. I shan't faint, or go into hysterics, and I shan't cry before you. Has any one done anything wrong?"

"Wrong! yes; but it's cruel to tell you, you can't help it. Lucy ought not to have sent for you."

"What has Harry been doing? I know it's Harry. What do these papers mean? Please to tell me the truth plainly; think you are speaking to some one on business, only don't use words that I shan't understand. Don't mind about my feelings; I want to understand everything."

"That's what we all want to do"—he glanced at the vacant chairs as though they were people—"and no one *can* understand, unless Tudor is here, and willing to explain matters."

"Do you mean to say that Harry is gone out of the way?"

"Yes."

"And the patent?"

"Curse the patent! Forgive me, Miss Tudor, but it makes one bitter to see a man throwing away a good certainty, and ruining himself and every one else for a chance."

Janet turned very pale.

"Will you explain what has happened? I have only heard from Lucy, and I supposed everything was prospering."

"Lucy is unreasonable, and won't understand. Poor girl, she has plenty to bear, I know. A married man has no right to be speculating."

"But about the patent."

"Which is utterly worthless, and always was."

"Harry did not know it?" Janet looked distressed and alarmed.

"No, I believe he was himself deceived; so far his fault was being too sanguine, but—"

Mr Leveson stopped.

"Tell me what you were going to say."

"Your brother led us to believe that the patent was paid for, and that the money we advanced was for machinery and alterations on the premises, and for the present current expenses of working it."

Janet was listening, almost breathless.

"It appears that the patent was *not* paid for; our money went to settle that account. Your brother owes for the machinery and alterations, and we have lost our money."

"What is it you don't understand? This seems plain."

"We don't understand how your brother has gone on being deceived."

"Perhaps he went on, hoping to make it answer."

"That's exactly what men always say in such cases; no one ever *means* to do wrong; the man who forges your name to a cheque means to take it up, according to his own account, in some instances really believes that he shall be able to do so, but it is a swindle all the same. Miss Tudor, I ought not to say this to you; I ought not to have gone into the subject with you; it is impossible to speak of such things without saying hard words, unfit for a lady's ear. Your brother, as soon as he found out that matters were going wrong, should have let us know; we would have cut short our losses."

Mr Leveson felt bitter. He was a young man who had had his way to make. He was looking forward to his own marriage, and these losses would put it aside indefinitely. He felt acutely for his sister, at the very time he called her unreasonable; if her husband had so little prudence, she might have a life of suffering. It is the way with some people, to find fault to hide deep feeling.

"If he deceived you about paying for the patent, I suppose it would be difficult to tell you how things were going on."

"There it was. The first deception is very often fatal."

"I'm glad I know about it; is this all?"

"All I know, except details and figures which you would not care to go into, and would not understand."

"What will Harry do?"

"Keep out of the way until we can make terms with his creditors."

"Does Lucy know where he is?"

"I think she does, I don't."

"What will they do when you've arranged with the creditors?"

"I can't precisely say, but your brother is a man sure to do something. This house must be given up."

"I must go and see Lucy."

"I wish you may be able to do more with her than I can. I know that she thinks me very cruel; but she either can't or won't understand the truth. I have not seen her since yesterday."

"Where is she?"

"In her own room."

"Janet went up-stairs, and knocked at the door of Lucy's room.

Lucy said "Come in."

She was sitting rocking herself to and fro.

"I sent for you, Janet; they tried to prevent me, but I knew that you would be kind; they're all against him." She leaned her head against Janet, and began to cry.

Janet kissed her, and tried to soothe her. Lucy wept on; this was her first great heart-wringing sorrow.

"Why didn't you come before?" The voice was fretful.

"I only received your letter very late last night."

"But you've been here, in the house, a long time. Mary told me when you came, and I've been waiting."

This was unlike Lucy; she was generally considerate and little requiring.

"I've been talking to your brother, Lucy."

"Then you know everything; and he's talked against poor Harry, but you love Harry, I know that; they can't set you against him."

"Dear Lucy, I don't think Mr Leveson would wish to set any one against Harry. I wanted to hear the truth."

"To hear the truth they must hear what Harry has to say. They've got his papers, and they say dreadful things of Harry, my brother does; and now that he wants help and money they won't lend him any; when they thought him rich he had plenty of friends."

"Did your brother explain everything to you?"

"No, I wouldn't hear. They wanted me to believe that Harry had deceived them. Cruel! they wouldn't have dared say it if he had not been in trouble."

Janet felt it difficult to know what to say. If Lucy was allowed to believe—rather, if she persisted in believing—Harry to be immaculate, she would be at war, in feeling at least, with her brother and every one. But it is almost as bitter a trial to cast down another's idol as to have one's own cast down.

"Lucy, do you think that Harry is perfect? Do you think that any one is?"

"No, not perfect, of course. But not being perfect is very different to cheating people. All Harry's friends are forsaking him now that he will be poor; *I* don't."

Janet was stroking her hand.

"Lucy, dear, I don't think people mean to be unkind to Harry because they don't wish to advance any more money. If the patent isn't worth any—"

"But it is, I know that it is. Harry wanted time and more money, and then I'm sure that it would have been right, and we should have been able to pay people, and I know that this will kill Harry."

"But, Lucy, why did not Harry let them know that—"

"I know what you're going to say. My brother has told you that Harry said the patent was paid for when it wasn't. I don't believe a word of it. Do you, Janet?"

"I'm afraid I must."

"Janet! How can you! You've only heard one side."

"I don't think it likely that these people would have invested their money, unless they thought the thing prosperous."

"And you think that Harry deceived them! You're as bad as the rest, Janet! I'm sorry I sent for you; I thought you loved him, and would help us."

"So I will help you, in any way in my power."

"Then why do you speak so unkindly of Harry?"

"I haven't spoken unkindly of Harry. God forbid that I ever should, or should even think unkindly, least of all would I say it to you."

Lucy stretched out her hand, and laid it on Janet's in her old fondling way. "Janet, I daresay I mistook what you meant. I've had so much trouble these last two days that my head seems bewildered. You don't side against us, you don't think that Harry has done wrong."

Lucy looked wistfully at Janet. If Lucy and Harry had been strangers, Janet would have given a great deal to have been able to give the desired answer to that look. Lucy had hold of her hand. Janet knelt down beside her.

"Lucy, if Harry should have done wrong, you could love him still? Knowing that people have done wrong need not prevent our loving them."

"I should love Harry always, of course, but you're putting me off. Harry has *not* done wrong. You're just like the rest. Oh! Harry, Harry, nobody will care for you but your wife. Janet, you're cold-hearted! You never loved any one! You've never known what sorrow is!" Lucy threw herself back in her chair and began to moan.

"Lucy!" Janet's voice was so earnest that it arrested Lucy's attention. Janet was not usually very demonstrative, but now two tears rolled down her cheeks. "Lucy! you don't know what you're saying. God forgive you, but long before I was as old as you I had known sorrow which almost broke my heart."

Lucy was moaning again.

"Lucy, do listen to me. I am *not* unkind to you, or to poor Harry either, but I want you to understand, and then you'll be better able to help him."

"What can I do?"

"I can't say at present, but before long, no doubt, there will be a great deal that you can do. Your brother—"

"It's of no use talking about him, he's all against poor Harry, and he's tried to set me, his wife, against him."

Janet was almost losing patience. What could she do with this poor unreasoning woman? Was it love, or denseness, or obstinacy, which made it impossible to make her understand that it was not incompatible with a wife's love and duty, and all kind feeling, to see where her husband had erred? Janet walked up and down the room for some time, and then she spoke very gently.

"Lucy, your brother did not wish to set you against Harry. Harry *has* done wrong. It's of no use to deceive you, or for you to deceive yourself. You *must* know it some time. You must love him all the same, and be kind to him. If you see where the wrong is, he will be less likely to do it again; and everything will be better when these business matters are arranged; it will all be better by and by, dear Lucy."

Janet went toward Lucy, and would have kissed her; but Lucy turned away. Lucy's was but a little mind, and by no means a clear one. Harry was in trouble, and in her idea it was heaping trouble on trouble, and showing a want of affection, to believe him wrong. She had heard of sunshiny friends, afraid of a cloudy day, and she was driving the converse into the extreme. When she turned away from Janet's kiss, she felt at war with her, and with her brother, and with all the world, at least her little world. She thought herself to be the only one who cared for Harry, the only one who loved him, and did him justice; she would fight for him. Poor Lucy! the brave feeling only lasted a minute; the next, and she was leaning back in her chair, and moaning piteously, "Oh! Harry, Harry, why did you go away! Why didn't you take me!"

Janet did not know what to do; her presence only irritated Lucy. She went down-stairs. Mr Leveson was still in the dining-room, busy with his papers.

"Well, Miss Tudor?"

"I can't do anything with poor Lucy, and she isn't fit to be left. It's of no use my staying; I only make her worse."

"I hope in a short time Tudor will be able to return; until then we must do the best we can."

"I'd have asked her to go back to Stoke with me, but I don't suppose she would now. She's offended with me."

"I expected she would be."

"I'll ask our old nurse, Grace, to come and stay with Lucy. I think that might do. Isn't there a coach by which I can return to Stoke this evening?"

"Yes, but you'd better stay until the morning; you'll be quite knocked up."

"I'd rather go."

Janet and Mr Leveson dined together; Lucy would not come down-stairs; and afterwards Mr Leveson walked with Janet to the inn, and put her into the coach which passed near Stoke.

CHAPTER XVI.

The country was in an unsettled state, and Holme felt the pressure of the times severely. Some of the factories were closed, and many others working short hours. The distress was spreading slowly but surely, from the mill-hands to various ranks of the community. The pressure was felt by all, but very unequally, even among those most liable to be affected by it. Mr Bateman and others of kindred minds had taught their men to look on them as friends; they recognized, and wished the men to recognize, that the obligation was not one-sided, but mutual. They paid fair wages, and then encouraged their people to be self-reliant, to put by something for a rainy day. These had something to fall back on. Mr Bateman did more than this; he was munificent in his donations to his own men, and to the general fund, now that the distress was great. He was not himself one of the merchant princes, but he gave with a liberal hand. It was his creed that gain and loss should go together; in other words, that if men in prosperous times, year after year, swept princely fortunes into their coffers, all derived from those mills and factories, that they should be equally princely in their charity when the evil day came, that it should be given by thousands, not by fifties and hundreds. If Mr Bateman could have had his way, he would have made the question a local one, he would have had no begging over England for the distressed operatives of Holme. He would have gone to all who were, or had been, connected with the factories, and would have said, These men, who are wanting, have realized for you princely fortunes, their labour has made some of you what you now are; in the day of their trouble it is you who must relieve them, we must not take the harvest to ourselves, and leave the labourers to be cared for by those who have reaped no benefit. If all had thought thus, there would have been but little distress in Holme, and no disaffection; as it was, the distress was very great. Money came in from all quarters; kind hearts did not stay to think whether it ought to be a local question or a national one; men and women and children were suffering, they must be fed and clothed; but there is an old saying, "While the grass is growing the steed is starving," and in spite of the efforts of feeling hearts the suffering was great, and by degrees the men in Holme became turbulent. Mr Bateman had nothing to fear, no one would harm him, but some among the less popular had received threatening letters, and the timorous were afraid to venture out.

The usual party, consisting of Aunt Wood, Aunt Delia, and Aunt Mary, with Uncle Jeremiah and Uncle Esau, sat at breakfast at "The Vale." Deborah brought in the letters, and left the room, and then she returned and said that that letter—and here she pointed to a dirty one written on coarse paper—had not come by post, but had been given her by a man, who said she was to be sure to give it to "Master."

Uncle Jeremiah opened that letter first, and, contrary to his custom, his face showed signs of emotion.

"What's the matter, Jeremiah?" said Aunt Wood, "you haven't lost money?"

"No." Uncle Jeremiah looked frightened, but offered no explanation.

Aunt Wood took it and read it. It was a threatening letter, purporting to be the sentiments of the workmen in Holme; it contained a general denunciation of tyranny, spoke of employers as tyrants, on whom the vengeance of the oppressed would fall, and it pointed more particularly to Mr Jeremiah Higgins, and intimated that unless he opened his work-shops immediately, and paid the men full wages, everything would be pulled about his ears.

"Humph!" Aunt Wood snorted, "an' you're frightened by such moonshine as that! Them as writes such letters ought to be hung, an' so they will be some day, an' serve 'em right."

"What about the letter? Let me see the letter," said Aunt Delia.

Aunt Delia looked at it, so did Uncle Esau and Aunt Mary.

"We ought to do something," timidly suggested Uncle Esau.

"What?" exclaimed Aunt Wood contemptuously. "Do nothing. They only wants to frighten you, Jeremiah, an' make you give 'em money. Them as talks don't act. If they'd wanted to harm you, wouldn't they have done it without telling you? You scared fool! does robbers come an' say, 'I'm going to break open your house such an' such a time?'"

"I believe we ought to do something," said Aunt Delia. "Esau's quite right. I've read dreadful things of the mob writing threatening letters, and then burning houses."

"Poor people!" said Aunt Mary, "I'm afraid they've suffered very much, and that makes them unreasonable."

"There you go," snapped Aunt Wood. "I believe you, an' Delia, an' Jeremiah, an' Esau, 'ud let anybody get your money from you; *I* won't."

"It wasn't us that sent Janet Tudor away, and brought that disgrace on the family," said Aunt Delia.

Aunt Wood did not speak for a few minutes; it was a favourite mode of silencing her.

"I wonder whether they'd come here or to the counting-house?" said Uncle Jeremiah.

"They won't come at all. If they did 'twould be to the counting-house, as any man o' your years, with any sense, might ha' known. 'Tis your money they want, not you, nor me. If they came, 'twould be 'cause they thought you'd got money there, an' they'd try to break open your strong box, maybe they might burn your books out o' mischief!" Aunt Wood had recovered from Aunt Delia's snubbing.

Uncle Jeremiah winced at the idea of those books, those much-prized green ledgers, with the copper-plate writing and flourishing capitals, being thumbed and soiled by the dirty hands of an angry mob; his imagination was more than usually lively, and he even pictured to himself his books as forming part of a bonfire in the middle of the dingy court into which the counting-house opened.

Uncle Esau thought of the beautifully bound books, in the carved book-case in his bed-room.

"I shouldn't like them to touch *my* books," he said, as if half afraid to hear the sound of his own voice.

"*Your* books! what 'ud they want o' toy-books like yours?" said Aunt Wood.

"What should they want with Jeremiah's?" said Aunt Delia.

"They *don't* want 'em," replied Aunt Wood; "an' I've told Jeremiah so, only he's so faint-hearted. They're only after money an' mischief."

"It would be just as much mischief to destroy Esau's books, or my dresses," said Aunt Delia.

There was nothing doing in the way of business; nevertheless from habit Uncle Jeremiah generally spent an hour or two each day at the counting-house. In spite of Aunt Wood's opinion that such precautions were unnecessary, he resolved to put his books in a place of safety.

The streets which he passed through were unusually quiet. Uncle Jeremiah was not very observant of such things, and this day, as he walked along, his mind was occupied with devising the best means of cheating the mob, in case they should attack the counting-house.

He went into the counting-house ; no clerks were there; there was nothing for them to do. The only person in attendance was a woman who kept the place clean, so far as it was kept clean, and lighted the fires. When she saw her master coming she went and stirred the fire in his office, and then went out to do her marketing.

If Jeremiah Higgins had been less engrossed with his own thoughts, perhaps he might have perceived that he was closely watched by two men. They were waiting for him at the outskirts of Holme, they kept him in view until he turned into his counting-house, and then they stationed themselves out of sight of the counting-house windows, just inside the archway which led into the court in which it was situated. They kept the door in view, that he might not leave the building without their knowledge. By and by the clocks from the churches struck twelve; they heard the clock in the counting-house strike also. They remained stationary some minutes, it might be ten; they looked at each other, and then one of them passed from the archway into the street and was lost sight of in some of the lanes and alleys with which that part of the town abounded; the other man kept watch in the archway.

Uncle Jeremiah looked at the books, those cherished books with the copperplate writing; he turned over the leaves fondly, looked tenderly at those columns of neat figures, much as a connoisseur would look at a folio of original sketches by old masters. Then he looked at an iron safe which stood by the window in his counting-house. If the mob came, that would be sure to attract their attention; it only contained papers, but they would be sure to break it open, thinking it contained money, and they might destroy the papers in wantonness. For a few minutes he thought of what Aunt Wood had said, and felt inclined to do nothing. Then he looked at his books again; the mob might destroy them; better to take too much precaution than too little.

Underneath the stairs was a dark closet, where the woman who swept out the counting-house kept fire-wood. Uncle Jeremiah recollected that in the corner of this closet was a trap-door, which opened on six steps, which led into what had probably been a cellar, but which had never been used since the place was a counting-house. He thought it very unlikely that any one would discover the trap-door; the closet was dark, and nearly full of firewood. The firewood was lying over the trap-door; he pulled it away and heaped it up in another corner. The place was so dark that he could not find the trap-door; he went back to the counting-house and fetched a lantern; the trap-door was opened by a large ring in the centre; it was all so covered with dust and dirt that it was some time before he could find it. At last he saw it. He pulled, and pulled, but could not move it; it was years since that door had been opened; the hinges were rusted, and set firm with dirt. Uncle Jeremiah pulled again and again; it did not feel so immoveable as at first; he perceived a slight vibration; at last the rusty hinges gave a shriek; after a strong pull the door flew back, disclosing a black-looking cavern beneath. Uncle Jeremiah went down the steps; the cellar was small, the air felt cold, and damp, and oppressive, and unwholesome; it was not perfectly dark, for at the other end there was a grating, about a foot square, which looked into a back street, coming level with the ground; on one side stood an old beer horse, the wood of which was decaying. Uncle Jeremiah returned to the counting-house for his books; he could only carry a few at a time. How good the warmth of the fire, and the air, and light, even of that dingy counting-house, felt, after the cellar! He had to make several journeys before all the books were carried down. He piled them up on the old beer horse. Then came the most difficult task, the moving of the iron safe; it was not clamped to the wall, but it was very heavy. He managed to drag it a little way from the wall, then he was obliged to stop and rest; he dragged it into the middle of the office, and then stopped to take breath and wipe his forehead. As he stood resting he fancied that he heard a confused sound, like the tramp of many feet. Surely they could not be coming! He listened again. There *was* a sound of voices. He made a great effort, and dragged the safe to the door of the closet; he was obliged to stop again, his strength failed him. He heard a rushing and a roaring, different from anything which had ever reached his ears before. He rushed back to the counting-house, the windows of which looked into the court. Through the narrow archway a multitude of men were pouring into the court, gesticulating and shouting; he heard his own name called out more than once. One man seemed to have some control over the mob, an untidy, reckless-looking man. Jeremiah Higgins recognized many of his own workmen in that crowd. He felt a deadly sickness come over him. He heard his name yelled out with oaths and imprecations. If they found him, would they not tear him limb from limb? His first impulse was self-preservation; the iron safe might be sacrificed; but when he saw it standing there by the cupboard door, it suddenly flashed across his mind that they might think he was trying to take it away, and that it might lead them to his hiding-place. He *must* move it, every moment's delay might cause him a horrible death. To his dismay, he found that he had piled up the fire-wood so that he could not get the safe into the closet. The court was full of people; he could hear that the back street was full also; there was no chance of safety but in concealment. He tore away the fire-wood, frantically threw it into the opposite corner. The mob filled the court-yard, in another minute they would be in the house. The lower windows were guarded with iron bars, and the door was bolted, but that could only occasion a short respite. Again he seized hold of the safe, dragged it to the steps, and pushed it down; it fell with a crash, and filled the place with dust which nearly suffocated him; it had crushed a gigantic fungus which was growing in the cellar. Jeremiah

Higgins started back, but the men were hammering at the door. He went down the steps, and closed the trap-door after him, just as he heard a shout of triumph from the mob; they had forced the door, and were pouring into the counting-house. He heard them rushing along the passage over-head, shouting and yelling. They seemed to be going all over the premises. Then there was a groan of disappointment; they were looking for him and could not find him. From the grating he could see the mob in the back street. He put out the light in the lantern, lest it should attract their attention. He crouched down in the darkest corner, listening and watching. To his horror, he saw a man stoop down and peer into the cellar through the grating; he was afraid the man saw him, for he spoke to another man, and then both look-ed in. He listened again, with strained attention, to the sounds above. There had been more shouting, and then a lull of voices; there seemed to be some dispute. Jeremiah Higgins could hear enough to guess that they were divided in opinion;

some thought he must have left the premises, and others thought he was still there.

"He's here somewhere," said one voice. "I watched the door myself, an' my comrade watched t'other; we saw him go in, an' neither of us ha'n't seed him go out."

"He's gone, for all that."

"He's not, I should ha' seed him."

"Let's burn the place, then we'll make sure of him."

"Smoke him out of his hiding."

The mob caught up the cry, "Burn the place!" "Burn the place!"

Jeremiah Higgins heard the cry, "Burn the place!" He crouched trembling in his corner; bitterly cold though it was, the perspiration stood in great drops on his forehead. He thought of the building in flames, and himself suffocated, perhaps roasted to death, in his hiding. Already he thought that he smelt smoke, and saw a thin vapour floating about the grating. How long he remained there, with every sense strained to the utmost, he could not tell; it might be minutes, or hours, or weeks, it seemed half a life-time. Then he became gradually conscious that the building was quiet, that there was no yelling, nor shouting, nor noise of footsteps; still he did not move, but crouched in his corner, and watched the grating, expecting to see those hideous faces peering in at him. There was the old mouldering beer-horse with his books piled up on it, and there was the iron safe, it had fallen on its side. So overstrained had been all his faculties, that the past two hours seemed all his life, and all before a dream. He was conscious of the intense cold creeping over him. As his eye became accustomed to the darkness of the place he could see that the walls were damp, and covered with green slime. He saw something in one corner move; he watched it until it came into the light, which streamed through the grating on to the floor; it was a large lizard wriggling along; it might crawl upon him, it turned towards him, he felt sure that it *would* crawl upon him; he loathed it, yet he felt powerless to go away, it was as if an irresistible power held him; there he remained crouching alone.

The mob had left the counting-house. The reason of their going so suddenly, and without doing any mischief, was that there was a rumour that Mr Higgins had been seen walking across the fields towards "The Vale." A boy had met him.

Either the boy did not know which Mr Higgins it was that those frantic men wanted, or he was but imperfectly acquainted with the two brothers. It was Uncle Esau that the boy had seen; he had walked part way with Uncle Jeremiah and had returned.

The mob proceeded as fast as they could towards "The Vale." As they came to a turn in the road there was a sudden halt; the furthest back shouted, and urged their leaders forward, but of these each as he advanced halted too, and looked at his neighbour.

At the turn of the road an unexpected sight met their eye, a glittering mass, moving rapidly along with great precision. Each man looked at his neighbour with suspicion; there must have been treachery. There had been no treachery, but an incautious word had been spoken before one of Mr Bateman's men, which had been quickly told to "Mr Andrew." Mr Bateman and his son feared nothing for themselves. What had been told them amounted to but little; but knowing the state of the times, there might be mischief for some of their neighbours; at any rate they ought to be prepared. Andrew Bateman rode to Salford the evening before, and the result of his journey was that a body of military marched into Holme, and met the rioters on their way to "The Vale." The ringleaders were secured without a struggle, and the others, crestfallen and spiritless, gradually dispersed.

At "The Vale" Aunt Wood and her sisters were ignorant of the danger which had been averted from them, and of the peril in which their brother Jeremiah had been placed.

Aunt Wood sat as usual knitting by the window. Aunt Delia was by the fire, and Aunt Mary was busily engaged cutting out a set of shirts for Uncle Esau, and placing in little heaps gussets, and collars, and wristbands.

"I wonder Jeremiah isn't home," said

Aunt Wood. "It's near upon dinner-time. Where's Esau?"

"Up in his room, I think; he didn't stay at the counting-house," said Aunt Mary.

"I can't think what Jeremiah goes there for, if there's nothing doing," said Aunt Delia. "I believe he likes those horrid great books."

"An' a good thing if he does; better than lolloping over the fire, making believe to read trash," retorted Aunt Wood.

Aunt Delia did not reply, but, as if in defiance of Aunt Wood, she drew her chair a little closer to the fire, and turned over the leaves of her book faster than usual.

Deborah burst into the room. "Oh! if you please 'm, is master come back? 'cause, if he isn't, the mob has been an' burnt the counting-house, an' they can't find master, though they've a-looked from the top to the bottom, an' if he isn't here he's burnt. Oh! dear, oh! dear, to think as I should live wi' a master as 'ud be burnt!" Deborah sank down on a chair in strong hysterics.

The three sisters looked at one another;

neither could speak. Aunt Wood was the first to recover herself.

"Stop that noise, woman, will you? Tell us what you mean. I don't believe a word. How can they have looked from the top to the bottom of the counting-house, if the place has been burnt!"

But instead of giving any further information Deborah got much worse, and was obliged to be carried into the kitchen. Aunt Mary followed, hoping to learn something definite.

Cook stood and looked at Deborah, but the source of the information was apparent; the baker's boy, with a bread-basket over his shoulder, was standing in the middle of the kitchen.

Deborah, on account of her hysterics, was regarded as an object of interest, if not a heroine, by the baker's boy and the scullery-maid. Cook wiped her eyes with her apron, and spoke in a whining voice; she felt herself wronged by Deborah monopolizing all the interest.

"Who told Deborah about Mr Jeremiah, cook?" asked Aunt Mary.

"Please, 'm, Mr Jones's young man, which is here, 'm. Ohoo—. Ohoo—." Cook showed signs of hysterics.

"Don't go into hysterics, please," said Aunt Mary. "I hope there is some mistake; but if your master should be hurt we shall want your help most likely."

Cook thought better of the hysteric business, under the prospect of being of importance in case anything should have happened to "master."

"Tell me what you have heard." Aunt Mary spoke to the baker's boy.

"Yes, 'm, they've a-been to the counting-house, if you please, 'm, an' a-broke ivery thing open, an' then a-burned it; an' they was a-coming here, only the milling-tary were upon 'm, which killed a hundred, an' is going to hang a lot where Mr Higgins' counting-house were, for an example like."

"Did you see them yourself?"

"No, 'm, but my sister's husband saw a man as did."

Aunt Mary became much more easy. The extreme improbability of the baker's boy's story, made her hope that there was but little truth in any part of it.

She went back to the parlour. "I can't make much out of the baker's boy; we must go to the counting-house."

Uncle Esau had come into the room whilst Aunt Mary had been in the kitchen.

"Was there anything like a disturbance when you were in Holme this morning?"

"No."

"You have the horse put in the gig, and I'll be ready to go with you in a minute."

Aunt Wood said, "Depend on it there's nothing in it; it's only them gossiping maids."

Aunt Mary and Uncle Esau drove into Holme, down the narrow street which led to the counting-house. They got out of the gig at the arch-way leading to the court. Outside everything looked as usual. They went into Uncle Jeremiah's office.

Uncle Esau pointed to the place where the iron safe had stood.

"Gone," he said.

"What's gone, Esau?"

"The safe, and the books too."

Aunt Mary looked round the room; so they were; she had not noticed it before.

The woman who swept the office came in.

"Where's your master?" said Aunt Mary.

"Master! Gone home, isn't he?"

"He's not at home, we haven't seen him since the morning."

The woman turned very pale.

"The mob comed here this mornin', shouting an' hollowing, when I wer' out, but they went away a' to a suddent, an' niver did no harm, an' a boy told me as how he'd seed master walking across the fields nigh 'The Vale,' so I 'sposed he'd gone afore they comed; he don't stay very long now, you know."

"Your master's *not* at home, he must be somewhere here."

They went all over the premises, into every place except the one in which Uncle Jeremiah was concealed. Neither Aunt Mary nor Uncle Esau knew of the cellar. There was the possibility of his having reached home since they had left, but Aunt Mary remembered what the baker's boy had told her of the rioters having come part way towards "The Vale," and she feared her brother must have fallen into their hands.

They drove silently back to "The Vale."

"Is Jeremiah come back?" asked Aunt Mary.

"No."

"What had we better do, Rhoda?"

Aunt Wood sat with her knitting in her hands, but doing nothing; a number of stitches had dropped off one of the needles.

Aunt Mary repeated her question.

Aunt Wood did not reply; she sat motionless, with glazed eyes, stricken with paralysis.

That evening the man and his wife who lived at the counting-house sat by their fire, talking over what had occurred during the day. The woman went to fetch some wood from the cupboard under the stairs; she had not been gone a minute when her husband heard a shriek, and she came rushing back into the room, declaring that she had seen a ghost in the cupboard. The man remembered the cellar; it was possible that his master might have hidden there, and now that all danger was over was coming out. He went to the cupboard, he saw that the wood had been moved. He was just going to open the trap-door, when it slowly opened, apparently of itself, and Jeremiah Higgins came out, half-frozen, and looking pale and scared. It was some time before the woman could be convinced that it was really her master, and not a ghost, which she had seen. Jeremiah Higgins felt his limbs so cramped and benumbed that he could scarcely stand. He could not believe that he had only been a few hours hidden in the cellar; it seemed half a life-time. He warmed his frozen limbs and had something to eat, and then the man went out and got a carriage and sent his master home to "The Vale."

CHAPTER XVII.

The Christmas holiday had just begun. Janet Tudor sat in John Harris's kitchen, putting her work-box to rights; she had had a general turn-out of all that belonged to her, because, as she said, she was too busy in school time to put things very neatly away.

Uncle Esau came into the house. He said abruptly, and without any preface, "Janet, you must come with me directly."

Janet looked astonished.

"Sister Rhoda wants to see you; she's very ill. Put on your bonnet directly; you needn't stop to take much with you, we'll send for your box afterwards."

Uncle Esau spoke more decidedly than was his custom. Before Janet recovered from her surprise she found herself by Uncle Esau's side in his gig. Grace tucked a shawl round her, and then went back, and stood on the door-step watching until they were out of sight.

"Very ill, is she?" said Grace to herself. "I wish she'd leave Miss Janet her money; an' she might, seeing it's no good to her where she's a-going."

Janet had heard that Uncle Jeremiah's counting-house had been attacked, and that Aunt Wood was ill, but she did not know that she was *very* ill. Uncle Esau was uncommunicative, or rather not very lucid; all his energy seemed to have been expended in coming so promptly to John Harris's to fetch her. As they drove up to "The Vale" they saw a carriage standing before the house, and just as they reached the door a solemn-looking personage came out, and seeing Uncle Esau he went up to him, and mysteriously shook his head.

Uncle Esau said, "Isn't Rhoda any better?"

"Wonderful constitution, my dear sir, wonderful! Most interesting case. Any other case, should have been able to calculate how long it would last. Wouldn't say that Mrs Wood mightn't partially recover; no hope however of the left side, I fear. Your very charming niece, Mr Esau, I presume." The doctor bowed to Janet. "I had the pleasure of meeting her once at Mr Dent's."

"Sister Rhoda wanted to see Janet," said Uncle Esau.

"Ah!" exclaimed the doctor, "sad meeting, very sad, I see many of them, very trying, very distressing to a sensitive mind, quite upsets me, I assure you, Miss Tudor, unfits me for my duty. A man of feeling oughtn't to be a medical man."

"It's as bad for a clergyman, isn't it?" said Janet.

"Hum, well, perhaps, but the wear and tear to a medical man's feelings is something frightful, I assure you. You'll see Mrs Wood greatly changed, greatly. She'll know you, however, Miss Tudor. We've brought her through nicely, nicely. Not another practitioner in Holme that I'd have trusted her to, though I say it—respectable men, very, not up to these critical cases. Good morning, Miss Tudor, good morning. I hope I shall have the pleasure of renewing our acquaintance on a less melancholy occasion."

The doctor got into his carriage and drove off. Janet and Uncle Esau went into the house.

Uncle Jeremiah and Aunt Delia were in the parlour when Janet entered.

There is a certain awkwardness in being with people whose relative is sick unto death, when that relative has always been disagreeable, and you have no regrets at their going to heaven. When with the invalid, the awkwardness vanishes; there is a solemnity in the presence of one on the borders of the unseen world, which overpowers minor considerations.

To Janet's great relief, Uncle Jeremiah was looking over some accounts, and Aunt Delia was very contentedly reading the newspaper.

Uncle Jeremiah shook hands with her.

"How do you do, Janet, my dear," said Aunt Delia. "How fresh you look, and what a becoming bonnet you've got on! Where did you get it?"

"Out of the shop at Stoke, and trimmed it myself."

"Ah! young people can make themselves look nice in anything. But you always *did* know how to put on things well."

Janet was going to inquire for Aunt Wood, when Aunt Delia began the subject.

"You'll see poor Rhoda very much changed, Janet; she's lost the use of one side; it's paralyzed, you know. I suppose the fright we had about Jeremiah brought it on, though you wouldn't have expected it of Rhoda, she doesn't seem to feel much generally. Take off your bonnet, Janet, and sit down by the fire, and warm yourself."

In about half an hour Aunt Mary came, and then Janet went up-stairs to Aunt Wood.

The room was so dark that she could see nothing at first.

"Draw back the curtain, Mary, that I may see her," said a voice from the bed.

It was difficult to believe that that poor helpless invalid could be Aunt Wood, hitherto so hard, so chary of her help to others.

"How long is it since you lived here, Janet Tudor?" said Aunt Wood.

"Two years, I think it must be," answered Janet.

"I was very angry with you when you went away. They all say 'twas my fault that you went. Do you think it was?"

"It was better that I should go."

"Mary, you leave me an' Janet a bit."

Aunt Mary left the room.

"Now, Janet, answer me. Was it my fault that you left?"

"I don't suppose I should have gone if you hadn't said what you did."

"Ay, we was angry both. You told me that your father, with all his faults, wouldn't stoop to meannesses as we did, an' I told you you was a beggar's brat as we didn't want,—something o' that sort, wern't it?"

"Yes, but you're ill now, and it's not

worth while remembering what either of us said."

"An' that's why I *do* remember it, an' why I sent for you. Things looks very different when one's ill to what they did when one were well. It's strange to lie like me, an' look back years an' years, an' see everything look so changed—what we thought right then, to look wrong now,—an' it's hard to tell what were right an' what were wrong; we was taught to do as we did, and thought it the right way to be respectable."

"Don't talk like that, Aunt Wood. You're not accountable to me. You were not obliged to maintain me here."

"I *must* talk; I might be speechless again, like I was when first I were took. Do you forgive me, Janet Tudor? I wern't very kind to you, an' I've said hard things of them as is dear to you. Do you forgive me that?"

"Yes, Aunt Wood, I *do* forgive you."

"Would you come and live at 'The Vale' again?"

"No; I'm comfortable where I am, and I like being independent."

"You wouldn't trust us again?"

"No, not that, but we think so differently about everything that very likely we shouldn't be comfortable; that was what I told Uncle Jeremiah when he came to see me."

Aunt Wood's face looked flushed.

"I'd better not talk any more to you, Aunt Wood, it's tiring you; I'll go downstairs, and come and see you again presently."

"Stay, Janet!"

Aunt Wood put up the one hand which she could use and rang the bell.

Aunt Mary came.

"Mary," said Aunt Wood, "ask Jeremiah for what I spoke to him about this morning."

Aunt Mary returned in a few minutes with a little slip of paper, which she gave to Aunt Wood, and then she left Aunt Wood and Janet.

"How much do you get for being a school-mistress? An' there's something else you do, isn't there?"

"Yes, I'm Mr Platt's organist."

"Well, how much do you get?"

"Forty pounds a year."

"An' you really works for that, an' gets it."

"Yes, how could I live otherwise?"

Aunt Wood remained silently looking at Janet for a few minutes.

"Though you *are* Fulk Tudor's child, an' are so proud, you're very like a Higgins in some things."

Janet did not speak.

"You *are* like a Higgins, Janet Tudor; you don't like to be told it, I can see it in your face, but you're like 'em in getting on. *My* father began life wi' ten shillin' a week, an' he died at "The Vale,' an' left all his children a fortin', besides the business."

"I never saw my grandfather."

"No, he died afore you was born. Harry was the only one of Jane's children that ever he saw. Now, Janet, we all wishes you'd live at 'The Vale'; we has our pride as well as others, we don't like your teaching them Stoke children. If we was poor, an' had to get on, like my father an' mother, I should say you was right to do it, an' it was a credit to you; but why should you be fagging when there's plenty of money to keep you, an' no other neveys an' nieces, but the Dents, besides yourselves, nor ever likely to be."

Janet was wondering what would come next, and thinking how she could escape living at "The Vale" without irritating the invalid, for she was very loath to give up her independent life.

"It's very unlikely as I shall be here long," continued Aunt Wood; "I might have a seizure any minit an' be carried; an' that's why I sent for you, an' made Esau promise to bring you directly. This bit of paper that Mary brought from Jeremiah is the receipt he got for the five hundred poun' he was obliged to pay for your father. I bought it of Jeremiah this morning. I'll give it you; an' likewise I've had it put in my will that you're to have forty poun' a year, which is what you gets at Stoke, on condition you lives here, unless you marries, which is very like, and then you're to have your money all the same."

The tears came into Janet's eyes. She bent down and kissed Aunt Wood, and would have thanked her, but Aunt Wood said, with something of her old manner,—

"There, that's enough. Don't thank me, only say you'll come. Jeremiah, an' Esau, an' Delia, an' Mary, all on 'em wish it, only they said they knew you'd not come, so 'twas no good to ask you, an' I thought you'd not refuse the poor helpless old woman. Say that you'll come, Janet."

"Yes, Aunt Wood, I will. But I mustn't do anything unhandsome to Mr Platt. I must stay until he can get another governess. He has always been kind to me."

"I don't want you to behave unhan'-some to Mr Platt; you must tell him about what I've said at once, an' if he can't get another governess directly, why, you must go back till he can; but that don't alter what I've said. There's the receipt, now your father owes *you* the money; an' you'll come here to live as soon as you can."

Aunt Mary came into the room to take Janet away; she thought talking so much would excite Aunt Wood.

"Janet 'll come an' live here, Mary," said Aunt Wood, "as soon as Mr Platt can suit himself with another governess."

CHAPTER XVIII.

Ever since the day when Dr Thorpe visited Holme the subject of their conversation came again and again into Mr Bateman's mind. The Doctor thought him prejudiced, he saw that. Was he not much more likely to form a correct estimate of a woman's character than was the Rector of Eckington? He was more a man of the world. The Doctor's profession might make him lean towards charity, it might make him hope that there was good where no good existed. Charity was a beautiful virtue, but it would not do charitably to think no evil, to take for granted that all was well, and then to find a large crop of follies, or something worse, in an only son's wife. No, no, the Doctor meant well, but he was mistaken, Mr Bateman could not be deceived here; he had been deceived once, he never would be again; and then he tried to dismiss the subject from his thoughts. But he could not; in the midst of his business the Doctor's quiet voice *would* be heard. Strange girl she must be, Mr Bateman thought; I don't understand her game, but she's playing a deep one, and she's taken in my friend the Doctor, and won him over to her side. Well, he's mortal, he's not the first of his cloth whose better jndgment has been warped by a pretty face. Again the subject was dismissed, at least Mr Bateman tried to do so; he became restless and irritable. Miss Tudor *might* love his son, he thought; Andrew was a good match, better than she had any right to expect. Dr Thorpe had spoken of her refusing a better, *that* was not mercenary certainly; there must be some mistake, women were difficult to understand. Mr Bateman did not for a moment think that he himself could be mistaken. Supposing he was—it was not likely, it was not possible—but *supposing* he was mistaken, and that Miss Tudor was all that Dr Thorpe believed her to be. Oh that Andrew had taken a fancy to any one else, any one even in a humble position, he would not have rejected. But that girl —the daughter of the man who had wronged him, who had deceived him,—to bid *her* welcome, to own that he had been mistaken, at his age to own that he had been in the wrong; of course he needn't own it in words, but his actions would give proof of his altered opinion. This would be wounding to the pride which lurks in most hearts, and elderly people cannot cast aside a cherished prejudice; rather it is treasured like comfortable old slippers, which neither chafe nor gall, but which invite repose. He thought that he really *should* like to see the girl; not that Dr Thorpe had convinced him of her goodness—oh dear, no, not one bit; and he distinctly said that to himself his opinion was quite unchanged, and would remain so, but having heard so much about Miss Tudor, he felt a curiosity to see her. He was not so young as Andrew, nor so soft-hearted as the Doctor, so he was not so likely to be taken in; besides, when he had seen for himself, the Doctor could not think him prejudiced.

So one spring morning saw Mr Bateman on the coach which passed near Stoke. Andrew of course did not know of the journey; what need to tell Andrew, when he was only going out of curiosity, and when his opinion remained unchanged? Now that he approached Stoke he began to ask himself how he was to see Miss Tudor; he could hardly call upon her; what reason could he give for his visit? He could scarcely claim the freedom of an old friend. He saw the grey tower of the church rising from among the cottages; he would go towards it, and see what kind of a place it was, and think what next to do. As he approached the churchyard gate he heard a hum of children's voices; it proceeded from the house opposite. *That* must be the school. No doubt but that she was there. The door was wide open. By standing a little to the left he could see the whole of the interior. There she was; he could see her distinctly. The children were reading their Scripture lesson; he could hear her correct their mistakes from time to time; then a tall boy stood just between him and her, and he could see her no longer. There was nothing which struck him as strange in seeing her so employed; she only looked like a lady visitor at the school. The lesson was over, and the children went to their places; then they all stood up and sang; he could distinguish her voice leading them. Had she ever sung to Andrew? What a rich voice she had! School was over; the children came rushing out. He heard her ask who would come to the church with her; a little curly-headed boy ran up and volunteered his services. Mr Bateman walked round by the end of the church; he did not wish to be seen then. He heard her playing. The door was open; he went quietly in and sat down on one of the benches. She was practising something new, and one passage seemed to puzzle her, and she tried it over several times. Then she played something which she knew. Mr Bateman wished they would play like that at the church he attended in Holme. She was a good musician, doubtless, but what of that? Though the man who has no music in his soul is said to be capable of a number of bad things, it does not follow that the converse is good. Mr Bateman thought he should like to speak to her as a stranger, perhaps she might not recognize him. He heard her shutting up the organ, so he went out into the church-yard. The day was warm, he was beginning to feel tired, he would inquire of her whether there was any inn in the place where he could rest.

She came quickly along the path, with a folio of music under her arm. There was more decision in her manner than when he had seen her last; she was her own mistress now, and she had plenty to do, more than she could have accomplished if she had not had a clear head to apportion her time, and a determined will to keep her to it.

Mr Bateman approached, and asked if there was any inn in the place in which he could rest.

She recognized him instantly; but did not suppose that he knew her in her school dress.

"No; I fear you will find no inn nearer than the next village." She saw he looked tired, so she added, "But I am sure that John Harris, at the little farm where I live, will be glad if you will rest there, and will give you some refreshment."

"You don't have many strangers here, it appears."

"Very seldom, indeed, unless they are Mr Platt's friends, and then of course they go to his house."

"You have a large school for so small a village."

"Yes, I think we have. Mr Platt is very anxious that it should prosper. There was none two years ago."

"Indeed! what became of the children?"

"I suppose they ran about; some of them went to a dame school."

"Don't you find teaching hard work?"

"Oh! I'm accustomed to it; use is second nature, you know."

"Use wearies some people."

"Those people who only like novelties, you mean; but that is an expensive taste; only rich people can afford to get weary."

"But people get weary, whether they

can afford it or not sometimes, don't they?"

"Tired with a day's work, you mean; well, they rest and go on again."

"No, weary, and give it up, and turn to something else."

"I daresay some do; but 'a rolling stone gathers no moss.'"

"They wouldn't become millionnaires, you think."

"I don't know anything about that; but I think they would never be worth much, they'd never accomplish anything great."

"Don't you? Some brilliant things have been rapidly executed, and there has been no time to grow weary."

"But before the power to execute them rapidly was acquired there must have been hard work to bring those powers under control, and to develope them."

They had walked on towards the school-room. He liked talking to her; there was a freshness about her which pleased him.

"May I see your school-room?"

"Oh! certainly, but there is not much to see; the parish is too poor to build a school immediately, but Mr Platt has done the best he could."

The room looked very neat. On Janet's little table were some wild flowers in a glass. She saw Mr Bateman looking at them.

"The children bring them to me, they know that I'm fond of flowers; sometimes I have much grander nosegays from their own gardens."

It was nearly school time. Involuntarily he shook hands with her. She went with him to the door.

"There," she said, "you can see the chimneys of John Harris's house; it is not far, and you can rest there, I'm sure."

Janet went back to her school duties; her thoughts wandered that afternoon, and she wondered whether Mr Bateman had left the village, and what he had come for.

Mr Bateman did not go to John Harris's, as Janet had suggested; he recollected that Dr Thorpe had said that she lived with Grace. Grace then would be at John Harris's, and would be sure to know him. He remembered her talkative, bustling ways, and did not at that moment feel disposed to encounter her. He sat down under a tree in the shady part of the church-yard. Either the Doctor was right and he was wrong, or she was a witch, and it was no use trying to withstand her; or he was an old fool, who could no more be insensible to the charms of a pretty face than younger men. He began to doubt his wisdom in coming there, and to remember a certain piece of advice, about keeping at the greatest possible distance from temptation.

He felt sure that she knew him at once. He liked the way in which she sought to make light of her work; she did not try to work on his feelings, quite the contrary. Dr Thorpe was right in saying that she had plenty of spirit. But her life must be one of drudgery. Poor girl! well, she was a nice girl, he might admit that, without wishing Andrew to marry her. Andrew could not marry all the nice girls. She *was* a nice girl and a pretty girl, yes, and lady-like, and she must be clever; she played uncommonly well; he would like certain nieces of his to hear her play; he hated that dum-dum of theirs from morning to night, and wished there was no such thing as a piano when they were in the house, but he could have listened to her for hours. A small organ would do for his dining-room very well. Then came the hum of the children's voices from the open door, as the breeze passed him. Say what she might, it must be laborious, wearying work. He wondered what they did at "The Vale" to make her go away, not that he was much surprised at her going; he knew them. But she was a plucky girl. He fancied, or tried to fancy, what she would say if he introduced himself as Andrew's father, but he could not fancy what she would say, because she was so different from most of the girls that he knew. Why did she belong to Tudor? If she had only been some one else's daughter, there would be no difficulty. What right had he to such a daughter, and why didn't he take care of her, the rascal! and not leave her to knock about in the world by herself like that?

He *would* own that Andrew had not been taken in as much as he expected. He felt that he would like to see her again very much. Why should he not speak to her as an old friend? She could not help her father behaving badly, poor girl, of course not; he need not quarrel with her; she wanted friends all the more, and he might be friendly, without wishing Andrew to marry her.

If any one had told Mr Bateman how much he would alter his opinion in a few hours he would have said it was impossible. He was an honest, upright man, who abhorred deception. He might err in judgment, he might be self-deceived, but he never intentionally deceived. Dr Thorpe might have argued with him, and no arguments might have convinced him, but when he saw Janet and talked to her there was that about her which made him feel that she was as truthful and as upright as himself.

The church clock pointed nearly to four. He thought she would be returning home soon.

He heard the children singing, and her

voice leading them as in the morning. Then the children came running out, and in little groups sought their different homes, or played on the green beyond the church. In a few minutes Janet came out, and walked quietly towards the farm. Mr Bateman passed out of the other gate of the church-yard; he saw a path which he thought must lead into the same road, but beyond the village. He reached the end of the path just as she was passing.

"Miss Tudor, I think we may meet as old friends."

She coloured.

"You did not recognize me this morning."

"Yes, I did; but I did not think that you knew me."

"I had not seen you for several years, but I knew you."

"I remember how kind you were when I was a little girl; I have a drawing-book now which you once sent me."

Why did she speak only of his kindness? Instead of dwelling on the bright side she might have said, When I was in trouble you would scarcely know me. Was it that she really did not think hardly of him, or was it consummate tact? This passed through Mr Bateman's mind.

"Did you find your way to John Harris's?"

"I did not try."

She hardly knew what to think. What *did* he come there for? What could he have been doing with himself?

They were close to the farm. She lingered at the gate.

She hesitated a moment, then she said,

"Will you come in now?"

She did not in the least expect he would, but he did.

Mrs Harris was in the house alone. Grace had gone to the next village on some business of her own, and Janet was glad she had, for Grace had asked more questions about Andrew than she cared to answer.

"I have unexpectedly met an old friend, who knew me when I was a little girl."

Mrs Harris curtseyed, and asked if Miss Janet was ready for her tea.

Janet said "Yes," and then ran upstairs to take off her bonnet.

Mr Bateman watched her pouring out the tea. It was pleasant to have a lady performing those little offices. He sighed; perhaps he thought of past days when Andrew's mother, a young woman, presided at his table. The house was dreary now; he and Andrew alone. He did not seem much disposed to talk. Janet did not know what to say to him, yet the silence was embarrassing. He turned suddenly towards her.

"How long is it since you have seen Andrew?"

Her heart beat fast, but she answered with tolerable steadiness, "I have not seen him for a long time."

"H—m—"

Janet was silent, and did not raise her eyes.

"He knows where you are?"

"Yes."

"Pray how did he know?"

"He heard in some way that I was at Eckington, and went there, and then he was told where I was."

"Does he write to you often?"

"Never."

"Why not?"

Why did he question her? She could hardly bear it, but she replied, "Because there is nothing to write about; he will not come here again." In spite of her effort to keep it back, there was a tear in the corner of her eye.

"I'll never see him again if he does not."

Janet looked up in amazement.

"He'll be here to-morrow, or he's no son of mine."

Still Janet did not speak.

Mr Bateman laid his hand on her shoulder. "Janet, you can forgive an old man; in fondness for his son he may have wronged you."

If any one had scolded Janet, probably the tear would never have fallen; as it was, there were a great many tears. Mrs Harris looked in to see if they wanted anything, and thought that Miss Janet must have heard some ill news; she didn't like to inquire herself, but wished that Grace would come back.

Mr Bateman could not at all understand why Janet, who had plenty of spirit, should show such weakness. He supposed it to be a peculiarity of woman-kind.

He must return by the evening coach, and it was getting late.

"He will be here to-morrow, you may be sure, and, my dear, you'd better give those children a holiday."

CHAPTER XIX.

Janet was less proud in her happiness than she had been in sorrow, for, without troubling herself about the obligation she would be under, she wrote a note to Mr Platt asking for a holiday.

Andrew came as his father had said. What he said, and what Janet said, and what they did, shall remain untold; it is very unkind to intrude on people at such times. Those who have passed through similar experiences can fill up the blank from recollection; and those whose experiences have not yet tended that way must be content to bide their time, or to make a fancy picture. All that passed was, without doubt, extremely satisfactory to Andrew and Janet, but in plain matter-of-fact, black and white, and read without the aid of rose-coloured glasses, it might look stupid.

The day was warm and sunny. After awhile Andrew and Janet strolled out across the common where the heather was beginning to put out its tiny bells; they sat down among the purple blossoms. A few tall fox-gloves were raising their stately heads, little blue butterflies were flitting here and there among the flowers, and high up in the sky, out of sight, a lark was singing. They remained silent for some time; perhaps they thought how lovely the scene around them was; perhaps they only felt that it was in harmony with happy hearts; but they remained silent—great happiness, like its opposite, despair, is silent, it needs no language to express itself in.

"Andrew, it seems wicked and unfeeling of me to be happy when I don't know what has become of my poor father." A sorrowful look came over Janet's face.

"I was thinking of him that very moment. Have you any clue to where he is?"

"Not the slightest; it is months since I

heard from him, and I feel sure that my last letters never reached him."

Andrew did not answer immediately.

Janet looked up, and said abruptly, "Do you know, I feel certain almost that he has returned to England."

"I have had the same thought myself."

"Have you? That *is* strange; but for the last few weeks the feeling that he is in England has been so strong that I have started at every knock at the door and listened, thinking that I might hear his voice."

"Not very likely that he would come without writing; besides, wouldn't he be more likely to go to Salford, thinking that Harry was there?"

"No; I think he would come to me. Andrew, you don't know all I fear. I fear that he has succeeded no better over there than he did here; if he returns he will be in want; every poor broken-down man who passes me I look at—it might be him. I *know* that he will come back some day like that. That was *one* reason why I seemed so obstinate, and chose to be independent. I know that I was very proud sometimes, and didn't like having to feel obliged to people; that was wrong, wasn't it?"

"Of course it was."

"Well, but, besides that, I used to think if he came back like I was saying, I could do what I pleased—help him—try to make him comfortable; and if—"

"And if you were my wife you wouldn't be so independent, but would have to ask me, was that it?"

"That wasn't the reason why I wouldn't consider you engaged to me. I don't think I ever should if your father hadn't altered his mind."

"Janet, if I didn't think you loved me very much, I should be jealous of your father, and jealous of your pride."

"Not jealous of my poor father."

"Yes, jealous of your father. I can't understand a man's being jealous in the general acceptation of the word; if a woman gave *me* cause for jealousy she might go, she wouldn't be worth being jealous of; but I can quite understand being jealous of any person or thing which monopolizes a wife's attention."

"Andrew, you think I have considered him more than you. I didn't mean to be unkind; he is poor, and unfortunate, and unhappy, and growing old, and you are young and rich, and have everything you can wish."

"I hadn't you."

"But you could have chosen some one else, and I thought most likely you would."

"You did *not*, Janet, neither did you wish that I should. Why didn't you judge me by yourself? You did not forget me; why should I forget you?"

"You're not a woman."

"You think men are less constant than women?"

"Yes."

"Well, there may be differences of opinion as to that, and it's not worth while arguing the matter now; but, Janet, you must know from your own experience, even at this moment, that the want of some one thing on which we have set our hearts, may make all other possessions valueless."

"Not valueless, Andrew," and she laid her hand on his.

"To me all the good things of life were

valueless. I do not mean to say that you are not happier now than you were a week ago, but I do mean to say that your happiness is very far from being as great as it would be if one other wish of yours could be attained."

"You would not have it otherwise? You would not wish me to be very happy and to forget him?"

"No, Janet, God forbid that you should forget him! Only don't enumerate people's sources of happiness as a set-off against the one thing which they have set their hearts on, yet do not possess; happiness cannot be weighed in balances like that. Not having the one thing does not only make the cup of happiness less full—if that were all we should have little to sorrow for; but the one want often changes the quality of the rest; like a drop of gall in the cup, it makes the whole bitter. Do you remember our walk by the river a long time ago?"

"Yes."

"Do you recollect what I said?"

"Yes, everything." Janet was looking

away, stripping the bells from off the heather.

"You told me of sorrows which you saw coming; some had already come. You did not like to bring troubles on me, and I said two can bear it better than one."

"I remember."

"Did I speak truly?"

"Yes, quite truly. But it's natural not to wish to bring trouble on those we love."

"Quite natural, supposing it were possible to avoid it, which it is not. If you have troubles, I *must* share them, whether you will or whether I will. It can't be prevented while love lasts. Do you think it can?"

"No, I suppose not."

"And which do you think will trouble me most, to have you with me to tell me of what makes you unhappy, to bear it with you if I can't remove the cause, or to know that you have troubles and are bearing them alone?"

"I know what you mean, Andrew."

"Well, Janet!"

Janet stripped more bells off the heath,

and pulled down a tall fox-glove and picked off the blossoms.

"Well, Janet, then I suppose I may consider it settled that you won't make 'The Vale' your home when Mr Platt has found another governess. I wonder when he will get one to suit him. I shall tell him he mustn't be too particular."

"I think he *has* one in prospect who may do. This morning I had a note from him, in answer to one I wrote last night asking for a holiday, and he said he had just heard of one likely to suit. She's coming next week, and he asks me to stay a few days to teach her his plans."

"I hope she *will* suit. Now about the troubles which we are to bear together."

"It was very strange that poor Aunt Wood should give me the receipt for that money; it was what I never should have expected of her. Last night, after your father left, it felt as if all the troubles were coming to an end; and doesn't this bright, beautiful day seem a good omen?"

"I hope it will prove so, Janet. Now,

supposing Mr Tudor should return, as you think he may."

"I must trust you, Andrew;" she looked wistfully into his face.

He put his arm round her and drew her to him. "Yes, trust me, Janet, in helping you to find where he is, and in helping you to bear the disappointment if we don't succeed; but for the rest he shall be indebted to none but yourself. You shall be able to help him as independently when you are my wife as you would have done if you had remained Janet Tudor. Do you recollect our conversation in the conservatory at your Aunt Dent's, the night of that party?"

"You were rather cross that night."

"I believe I was; I didn't wish you to remember that; I shan't be cross when you're my wife. But I asked you if you'd have me, supposing my father could be induced to give his consent, but supposing he left me nothing, and you said 'Yes.'"

"So I would."

"I don't for a moment doubt it. From that time I saved all I could, and invested it well. I thought it possible that my father might say some day, 'Well, I won't refuse my consent, but you won't have a shilling from me; see if she'll have you now.' I should have acted on this, and I should have had a home for you, though not exactly such a one as I could have wished. I don't want this money now to make a home for you, because the old house will be ours, and I shall have what my father intended for me whenever I married, supposing he liked my wife. You shall have this money that I saved, Janet, to spend as you like; I shall settle it on you, and shall have nothing to do with it further than seeing that it is paying you good interest. I don't mean it to buy bonnet-strings and such like, but if your father should return you won't have to ask me for money; it will be your own, you know."

Janet did not thank Andrew; she did not speak for a long time; she thanked him in her heart, and loved him too much at that moment to say a word; but he understood it.

"I am going to buy a small house which stands at the end of our garden with some of your money, Janet. I've wanted it for some time, but it was not for sale before. It's rather out of condition now, but I shall have it done up. The people who are in it now keep it very untidy."

"What am I to do with a house, Andrew?"

"Why, you must give the present tenants notice to quit, and I will have the place cleaned and repaired, and then my father must rent it of you; it will do for some of his superannuated people. There's the old gardener, who can just creep as far as the green-house, and pick off a few dead leaves; he and his wife can live downstairs, and up-stairs there are three rooms; my father will be sure to want them for some old clerk; and we must have some creepers growing over the walls, and then it will look rather well from our windows, instead of being unsightly, which it is now."

"Oh! Andrew, I'll let the old people live there; I shan't want your father to pay me rent."

"I see that I shall have to look after your money; my father may as well pay you rent as pay any one else."

"Andrew, do look at your watch, I'm

sure we must have been here for hours; the sun was over our heads when we came first, and now he is all over there."

"It's five o'clock. Grace will wonder what has kept us so long."

"Oh! she'll guess. Mrs Harris told her that your father came yesterday, and that she was sure that something was the matter, and then I—"

"You told her a little more."

"Yes, it wasn't wrong. Grace isn't like a common servant; she has been a kind friend to me ever since I was a child."

And so they walked on towards John Harris's.

CHAPTER XX.

Mr Platt's new governess did tolerably well; at least he could not with an easy conscience be too particular when he knew that Janet's marriage was only delayed until he should be suited.

The Uncles and Aunts at "The Vale" were all extremely pleased with what Niece Janet was doing, and expressed their satisfaction according to their different dispositions. They wished her to come and stay at "The Vale," and Uncle Jeremiah and Aunt Delia would like to have given her a very grand wedding. Mr Bateman would also have liked a grand wedding for his son; he attached some importance to certain traditions respecting marriage feasts and wedding garments. But Janet said, "No; after we're married we'll be as grand as you like, Andrew, but let the wedding be very quiet; considering the humble position I have been obliged to fill, and also all that attaches to my poor father's name, it is better so, a gay wedding would seem heartless." And when Andrew told his father, Mr Bàteman said, "She's right, Andrew, she's always been a sensible girl, and good fortune has not turned her head." She went to "The Vale" several times for a day or two, to go shopping in Holme with Aunt Mary and Aunt Delia. Every one was very liberal to her, and Uncle Jeremiah and Aunt Delia added some costly presents, because they wished her to do them credit on entering Mr Bateman's family. Aunt Delia's great care was a white silk dress, with Brussels lace flounces, about the fashioning of which she worried the dressmaker unmercifully. She called it the wedding-dress, but Janet had not the slightest intention of being married in it. Uncle Esau went shopping with them sometimes. He would have bought all manner of expensive useless articles if Janet would have let him. His sisters told him that they would see that she had everything that she was likely to require, and that he should pay his share of the bills; but this did not fully satisfy him. He drove into Holme one day alone, and came back with a great cube-like parcel by his side. It was a huge work-box for Janet, the largest he could meet with, fitted with all kinds of work materials; the thimble, and pencil-case, and bodkins were gold, so were the bows of the scissors; one of them came off very soon, and the scissors never would cut. Aunt Wood would like to have given Janet a quantity of house linen, which she said, according to the opinion of her family, "was the most respectable present to make to young people as was setting up for themselves," but as Mr Bateman had got everything, 'twould be no good; this not being required, she would like to have knitted a number of worsted stockings, which would have been perfectly useless to Janet unless she had given them away to poor people. But Aunt Wood lay paralyzed, and could only use one hand; nevertheless, she wished to give Janet what she considered a respectable present peculiarly her own. She sent for Uncle Jeremiah one day, and she sent for her receipt-book; it was bound in green vellum like his ledgers, and it had brass clasps; it looked like a half-grown ledger. This book contained directions for making those pickles and preserves which stood on the store-room shelves. To say that Aunt Wood prized that book is saying little—she *believed* in the book; that green vellum book with brass clasps, and filled with crabbed writing, was to Aunt Wood beyond price. Uncle Jeremiah stood by his sister's bed-side. Aunt Wood held the green vellum book with clasps in the one hand which she could use. "Jeremiah," said Aunt Wood, "I sent for you about this book; it's no use sending messages by Deborah; servants forget. You have a book made exactly like this, not bigger an' not smaller, an' with brass clasps, an' you make the best writer you have among your clerks to copy all as is in my book into the new one; mind he dots his i's, an' crosses his t's, an' makes han'some capitals; an' mind no hurt comes to my book; you'd better cover it with writing-paper—folks is careless sometimes, an' a spot of ink might come on the cover; an' you'd better lock 'em both up in your strong box every night when you leaves the counting-house. It's for Janet Tudor I want it, so it must be done directly. Andrew Bateman's mother have been dead so many year that I don't suppose they've got a receipt-book in the house; no one knows the trash an' unwholesome things they eats in their pickles an' preserves." Uncle Jeremiah most likely attended to his sister's wishes, for a green vellum book with clasps was among Janet's possessions.

One bright June morning Janet was very quietly married at Stoke. She did not wear the grand dress which Aunt Delia had provided, but a fresh white muslin and a straw bonnet. It was a fancy of her own that she would have nothing inconsistent with her position as village school-mistress until she was Andrew's wife; but she had in her hand a bouquet of white flowers and maiden-hair fern, which Dr Thorpe brought from Mrs Darrel the morning of the wedding. Dr Thorpe gave her away, and Mr Platt read the service. The wedding company were only Mrs Platt, and Andrew's father, and John Harris, though the church was nearly filled with villagers. John Harris said the "Amens" very loud, and meant them. Mrs Harris and Grace, in new caps and gowns, were waiting their return from church. Mrs Harris was in a flutter of excitement, for, as she confided to Grace, "it reminded her of her own young days thirty year agone."

The knowledge people have of our private affairs is surprising, and the interest they manifest in them is still more astonishing. Andrew and Janet believed that they were being married very quietly, and that no one troubled himself about them. They were quite mistaken. People talked about them a great deal, knew a great deal that they did not know themselves, and the very quiet wedding did not make them say the less.

"It's shocking! isn't it, my dear?" whispered gossip number one to a dear friend. "He's going to marry a village-schoolmistress, quite a common person. Of course no one will call on her."

"Of course not," said number two.

"I don't believe it," said number three.

"It's breaking his father's heart," said number four.

"Poor dear Mr Bateman! It's dreadful for him in his old age to have his son make such a disreputable marriage," said number five.

Number one took up the parable, and said that the elder Mr Bateman, being broken-hearted, was about to give up business, sell his house, leave his money to a hospital, and depart this life.

An old young lady said. "Poor dear man, he wants some one to comfort him."

Number two returned to the charge, and said, "Mrs Darrel of Eckington patronizes the school, and the governess had the audacity to try and catch Mr Darrel, as if he'd have taken notice of such a one as her! Mrs Darrel threatened to expose her."

Number four knew for a fact that Mr Bateman went to Stoke and offered the girl a thousand pounds to get rid of her.

"And poor Mr Andrew is looking *so* ill," said number five. "What a wedding for Mr Bateman's son! I can't help pitying the young man, though he is so foolish. He'll be sure to suffer."

"Serve him right," said a lady who wore black silk mittens, and cherished a pug dog and a shrieking parrot, and had china monsters and kindred abominations on her cheffonier.

"And it's all false, every word you're saying," said a fresh little damsel, still in her teens. "You oughtn't to speak ill of your neighbours, and you're talking of what you know nothing. Miss Tudor is *quite* a lady, and I like her, and I hope she will be happy, and Aunt Darrel and Cousin Edward like her very much, and we wish she had married Cousin Edward; and I'll tell Aunt Darrel what you say, for it's a wicked story."

Janet and Andrew enjoyed themselves, being quite unconscious of what was said. They travelled about for a month or two, and at the beginning of autumn settled down very comfortably in Mr Bateman's old house. The five gossips all called upon Janet, so did the possessor of the china monsters, and they all ate bride-cake, and drank the bride's health, and wished her every happiness.

Next to their powers of invention, the most astonishing thing to observe, is the facility with which people change their opinion.

Gossip number one discovered that Janet was a distinguished-looking woman. "And how remarkably well she looks in that white silk, and the flounces are *real* Brussels!" she whispered to her dear friend.

"And what a nice thing for dear old Mr Bateman, to have his son so well married; what a comfort it must be to him to have a lady at the head of his house!" said number two.

"And you know, my dear," said number three, "the Tudors are a *very* good family, for all Mr Tudor was unfortunate."

"And, no doubt," said number four, "but that her mother's family will leave her something handsome."

"And it's been *quite* a love-match," said number five.

"You know she refused Mr Darrel of Eckington."

The lady possessor of the china monsters

was contumacious, and refused to believe that Miss Tudor had ever had the chance of refusing such an offer; whereupon the five gossips flew at her, and told her that people like the Darrels didn't care for money, and that the Tudors were as good a family as themselves, and that if *some* people, and here they looked hard at the possessor of the monsters, if *some* people had never had such chances, and wouldn't have refused them if they had, it was no reason why Mrs Andrew Bateman should not have had the one and done the other.

Janet would have been very happy in her husband, and in her home, but Andrew had said truly that one bitter drop may embitter the whole cup; her own family were that bitter drop.

Harry had left Salford. The nice house and handsome furniture was sold, and he was in London with Lucy, experiencing daily mortifications; mortifications which he would not have felt if he had cared less for appearance. As Mr Leveson had told Janet, Harry would find some employment; he did, and he was industrious. His poverty was but comparative; he never suffered privations, but it was bitter mortification to live in a tiny house, and to see Lucy without her pretty, expensive surroundings; it was the penalty he paid for a long time for beginning where he ought to have left off. It was up-hill work for a time to supply even this with a sullied character, but the hardest of all was, when he really honestly was trying to do the thing that was upright, to be doubted, and to have old transgressions flung at him, because some *could* not, and others *would* not, believe. For a long time even Janet could not be satisfied that he was doing right; she felt like one walking over insecure ground, never sure when a secret mine might not be sprung under her feet, and something hideous be disclosed.

Tom was still less satisfactory. He gave up his profession, or it gave him up. He wrote plausible letters accounting for the change, and saying how much he could earn by his pen. He spoke of leading periodicals with which he was *going* to be connected; he wanted a little ready money until his payments were due—would Janet lend it? Janet did lend again and again, until she could lend no longer. Tom's payments never *were* due. When she could send no more, Tom felt aggrieved; people who systematically borrow and hang on others always do; he took it as a right, and, as a matter of course, forgot past kindnesses, and felt wronged that the supplies were stopped. He wrote Janet a harrowing letter, reproaching her for living in luxury whilst he was starving. Andrew found her hiding her face on the sofa in her room in an agony of grief; he read the letter, comforted Janet, and wrote to Tom, telling him that if he possessed one spark of manly feeling he would not harass his sister, and desired that all applications for assistance should be made to himself. Andrew offered to procure Tom some situation, but intimated that it would be such as would necessitate his working, for that in that neighbourhood there were no sinecure berths. Tom, finding that Andrew had taken the matter in hand, knew that it was hopeless for him to think of being maintained in idleness. He felt no desire to accept Andrew's offer, but he really did bestir himself, and earned enough by his pen to keep himself in tolerable comfort; but he always spoke of Andrew as a hard-hearted, close-fisted man, who was making Janet as bad as himself.

Of Mr Tudor they heard nothing. For a long time they could get no clue to his whereabouts, and Janet silently sorrowed.

"I want you to come and see the cottage at the end of the garden, Janet—*your* cottage. I've had it cleaned, and painted, and papered; now it must be furnished."

They crossed the garden and went into the cottage.

"Oh! Andrew, how different it looks! It was such a horrid little den when I saw it before."

"So much for cleanlinesss."

"Really, Andrew, it looks so nice that I should like to live in it. What a dear little kitchen!"

"Now I think that the kitchen, and back kitchen, and the room beyond, will do for the old gardener, and up-stairs I thought we could put one of the old clerks who cannot work."

They went up-stairs.

"Andrew, this is more changed than

the down-stair rooms; what a pretty paper; and how pleasant our garden looks from the window!"

"I'm glad you like it. Now I want you to furnish it comfortably; not expensively, but comfortably."

"I shall like to do it very much. I'll choose a carpet this afternoon, and see about its being made."

While they were talking a servant came and gave Andrew a letter. It was only a tradesman's circular, but Andrew, after looking at it, crushed it up and put it into his pocket."

"What is it, Andrew? Let me see," said Janet.

He took it out of the envelope and gave it to her, but put the envelope back into his pocket.

She glanced over it. "The newest novelties of the season! Is that all?" and she threw it away.

"Well, then, you'll do what I asked; see to the furnishing."

"Yes; come with me and choose the carpet."

"No, I can't this afternoon."

"I'll leave getting it till to-morrow."

"You'd better get it to-day, if you're at liberty."

"Why, Andrew, there's no hurry. One would think that the old clerk was waiting to come in."

They returned to the house. She put on her bonnet to do Andrew's bidding, and Andrew went out by himself. He walked quickly till he reached the draper's shop from whence the circular had come; there he went in.

"I want to speak to Mr Popham."

Mr Popham came forward, rather surprised. Andrew went with him into a little back room behind the shop.

"A circular came to my house to-day in that envelope; who directed it?"

"Well, sir, nothing wrong, I hope, sir," said Mr Popham, rubbing his hands.

"Nothing wrong; but I want to know who directed it."

"Well, sir, you see when we're busy, and have a lot of these to send out at the change of the season, we generally employ some one to direct them, and to get them ready for us. I haven't employed this person before, sir, but his name's Smith, a very fair-seeming, pleasant-spoken man. But I hope there's nothing wrong, sir, because, if there is, I assure you I know nothing of it; we can't be answerable for every one we employ in this way."

"There's nothing wrong; you needn't alarm yourself, Popham. Where does this Smith live?"

"Well, a long way from here. It's in that new neighbourhood that they're building quite the other side of the town. Charlton Street, number 17, is where Smith lives. Not a very pleasant place."

Andrew went to Charlton Street. It was situated in a dreary, newly-built neighbourhood, as Mr Popham had said; the dreariest-looking of all—a new *poor* neighbourhood. There were rows of dirty, slipshod-looking houses, with many scarlet-curtained windows, from whence came fumes of tobacco-smoke and spirits, and where greasy, sodden-looking men lounged. Andrew threaded that labyrinth of unwholesome streets until he came to 17, Charlton Street. He stayed there a long time, and he went there the next day, and the next, but he never told Janet where he had been, or what he had seen. That one secret he kept from her always. After one visit to Charlton Street he said, "Janet, do you think you could get the cottage ready by to-morrow?"

"To-morrow, Andrew, that *is* short notice; but I'll try. The carpet is down, and the curtains are up."

"Do you think you *can* make it quite comfortable by to-morrow?"

"Yes, I think I can."

Janet was as busy as possible all the next morning, superintending the arrangements in the cottage. Andrew came in to look at it.

"Well, Andrew! What do you think of it? *I* think it looks most comfortable."

Andrew said nothing, but he kissed her.

"How pretty our garden looks from this window! I've charged Mrs Clarke to have the fire burning bright, and I'm going to gather some flowers to put on the table, they make a place look homish, you know, as though there was someone to care for you. The other room is quite as comfortable as this; come in and see it. But who is it that's coming? You've told me nothing about him, Andrew. Is he *very* old? Was he a clerk of your father's?"

"He was in my father's employ."

"Andrew, I don't think the old gardener's wife can wait on him, she's getting old, you know. I've been talking to her about her granddaughter, she's a strong girl; I think we must have her to do the hard work."

"Do, if you like."

"Andrew, you've not told me his name; the old man's who's coming here, I mean."

Andrew was looking out of the window. "That mass of chrysanthemums looks well in our garden, doesn't it?"

"Yes. Dear me! it's lunch-time, and my hands are *so* dirty. I must gather my flowers after lunch, and then I want to go into the town. Are you going out?"

"Yes, dear, but not with you."

Janet gathered her flowers, and gave many injunctions to Mrs Clarke about keeping up the parlour fire, and then she went shopping in Holme, and came back just in time for dinner. Andrew had not returned, but she saw him crossing the garden while she was taking off her bonnet, and he was in the dining-room when she went down-stairs.

"Well, Andrew, does the old clerk like his cottage?"

"How do you know that I've been to the cottage?"

"I saw you crossing the garden."

"He likes it, I believe. After dinner you must go and see him."

"Me!"

"Yes, you."

"You'll come to."

"Very well; but are you becoming shy?"

"No, but I shan't know what to say to him."

"Say that you hope he likes the cottage and finds it comfortable."

Dinner was over, and Andrew's father had retired to his arm-chair by the side of the fire for his nap.

"Now, Janet, will you go?"

"Yes, if you'll come too."

"Put on your bonnet, you'll find it cold crossing the garden."

"No, it's not worth while."

There was a gust of wind when they opened the garden door. Andrew put his handkerchief over her head.

They knocked at the door of the cottage. Mrs Clarke opened it.

"I kep' a *very* good fire, ma'am, as you said, an' everything looked as comfor'able as possible."

They went up-stairs. Andrew opened the parlour door; she thought he came in with her, but he did not, he turned back to speak to Mrs Clarke. There was a figure sitting in the arm-chair by the fire; the hair was slightly grey. She trembled exceedingly. She had thought to see a stranger, and instead she saw a well-remembered face. She was at his side, and her head was resting upon his shoulder, and as in years gone by, when in her childish way she sought to comfort him, there was unutterable love in the one word "Father," which was all she could say.

It was a long time before Mr Bateman would recognize the occupant of the cottage. But one Christmas Eve, when Janet had gone to see her father, as they sat by the fire, the door opened gently and Mr Bateman entered. He went up to Mr Tudor and held out his hand, "Because—" he said, laying his other hand on Janet's head— "because of the blessing which has come into my house;" and when the workmen came for their Christmas gifts, and to sing their Christmas carol, Andrew and Janet and two grey-headed men were sitting by one fireside.

There was one old man who loved children, and whom all children loved; who would take them on his knee and tell them wild elfin stories; an old man whom the young who were not children loved also, and if he saw such letting slip the golden moment of opportunity he would humbly, oh! so humbly, tell them of a wasted life, that if, as he said, he should be permitted to rescue a thoughtless one, even then he would not deem his life quite lost.

When Mrs Clarke became feeble Grace came to live in the cottage, overjoyed to wait on her old master, "who," she told every one, "were the best master in the world; an' if it hadn't been for them Higgins's, things wouldn't ha' happened as they did happen." Grace was a terror to the little Batemans, whom she was perpetually counselling to behave like young gentlemen and young ladies, but of whom she was very proud.

John Harris was shy of coming to see Janet, "'cause," as he said to his wife, "it might look as though he wanted to be paid." Finding he *would* not come, Janet waylaid him in the market and brought him home with her, to the exceeding horror of one of the gossips, who "met Mrs Andrew Bateman walking with *quite* a common man, and talking familiarly to him."

And there was a blind man who came and played wondrously sweet music on the organ in the dining-room. Janet was sad after his visits, until after a time a fresh young face came with him. The young lady who defended Janet from the attacks of the five gossips had managed to console "Cousin Edward;" but there were two or three songs which "Cousin Edward" persisted that no one could sing like Mrs Andrew Bateman.

THE END.

CPSIA information can be obtained
at www.ICGtesting.com
Printed in the USA
LVHW110812120522
718525LV00003B/71

9 783375 003395